New Tales
of Mystery and Crime
from Latin America

New Tales
of Mystery and Crime
from Latin America

Edited and Translated by
Amelia Simpson

Rutherford ● Madison ● Teaneck
Fairleigh Dickinson University Press
London and Toronto: Associated University Presses

Associated University Presses
440 Forsgate Drive
Cranbury, NJ 08512

Associated University Presses
25 Sicilian Avenue
London WC1A 2QH, England

Associated University Presses
P.O. Box 39, Clarkson Pstl. Stn.
Mississauga, Ontario,
L5J 3X9 Canada

The paper used in this publication meets the requirements
of the American National Standard for Permanence of Paper
for Printed Library Materials Z39.48-1984.

Library of Congress Cataloging-in-Publication Data

New tales of mystery and crime from Latin America / edited and
translated by Amelia Simpson.
   p. cm.
  ISBN 0-8386-3453-2 (alk. paper)
  1. Detective and mystery stories, Latin American—Translations
into English. 2. Latin American fiction—20th century—Translations
into English. I. Simpson, Amelia S., 1952– .
PQ7087.E5N49 1992
863′.08720898—dc20   90-56416
                                                  CIP

For Charles,
a minha mais completa tradução

Contents

Acknowledgments

Introduction   11

The Crazy Woman and the Story of the Crime
RICARDO PIGLIA   23

Hierarchy
EDUARDO GOLIGORSKY   31

Doctor and Doctoring
LUIS ARTURO RAMOS   36

Monday's Heads
IGNÁCIO DE LOYOLA BRANDÃO   46

Deposition
PAULO RANGEL   56

Mandrake
RUBEM FONSECA   62

The South Bay Crime
GLAUCO RODRIGUES CORRÊA   89

The Man under the Ceiba Tree
ARNALDO CORREA   148

Acknowledgments

For permission to publish all works in this volume by each of the following authors, grateful acknowledgment is made to the holders of copyright named below:

Ricardo Piglia: "La loca y el relato del crimen"; Eduardo Goligorsky: "Orden jerárquico"; Luis Arturo Ramos: "Médico y medicinas"; Ignácio de Loyola Brandão: "As cabeças de segunda-feira"; Paulo Celso Rangel: "Depoimento"; Rubem Fonseca: "Mandrake" (© 1979); Glauco Rodrigues Corrêa: "Crime na baia sul"; Arnaldo Correa: "El hombre de la ceiba"

Introduction

The reader of these pages is likely familiar with various types of mystery and crime fiction, especially the two major branches—the classic whodunit and the hard-boiled—and thus brings to the present book a set of expectations. From the armchair pulled close to the fire on a cold, wet night, the whodunit affords a view—almost pastoral in its tidy control of the natural elements—of a pleasant, innocuous world. Corpses are shunted on- and offstage with decorous efficiency so as not to detract from the distraction provided by a cast of more and less curious characters whose function is to drop hints until the teacup is full and sometimes running over. All along we know that truth will prevail and justice, as embodied in such social institutions as law enforcement agents and the courts, will triumph. The hard-boiled novel, on the other hand, begins and ends with a different premise. Here, a brave and relatively untarnished figure will prevail in spite of a bookful of gangsters, corrupt politicians and police chiefs, depraved business moguls, spoiled nouveau aristocrats, psychotic enforcers, and lowlifers of all sorts. Less tony than the whodunit, the hard-boiled still wraps it all up at the end, if only in the sense of showing the miserable state of things. Mix the two formulas, add to the detective's role that of principal suspect wanted dead or alive by the cops but only dead by the real culprit, send the whole crew off to exotic locales and social milieus, plant a clue in the fourteenth century, make the detective a feminist, a rabbi, an antinuke activist, a Navaho, or gay to give the plot a contemporary spin: most of the variations of the genre are accounted for or can be readily imagined. There are exceptions, and, in any case, predictability is a trait in many ways desirable and, beyond a doubt, desired.

How does Latin American crime fiction fit into the picture? There exist numerous detective stories and novels from Latin America that closely follow the patterns outlined above and, as

such, are, in a sense, superfluous. Latin American readers' resistance to such works provides perhaps the best testimony to this
circumstance. As publishers in Buenos Aires, Rio de Janeiro, and
Mexico City rhetorically ask, why publish a local author when a
translation of Agatha Christie is sure to sell and somehow make
more sense as well. Latin American readers are willing to accept
both the rules and the inevitability of the final score—however
improbable—when the game is played in London or Los Angeles.
Yet at home the genre does not comfortably apply. Reader con-
ditioning, which is formed by market practices and in turn influ-
ences those practices to a considerable extent, has led to diffi-
culties in matters as superficial as the choice of names and places.
"One of the rules of the genre," writes one Latin American author, "is the Anglo-Saxon setting. A detective named Rodríguez
'doesn't work' for the reader; if his name is Wesley, he 'works'
perfectly well."[1] Jorge B. Rivera asks us to consider the problems
of applying the genre to "a society where the police follow different *modus operandi,* where the private 'detective' is practically
nonexistent, where there is no trial by jury . . . ," as we know it.[2]
The same author sees crime fiction as a form "anchored to or
typified by a specific production apparatus, a certain 'local color'
and certain contextual relations (economic prosperity, for example), which are absolutely exogenous."[3] To appropriate the genre
and nationalize it by making it Brazilian, Argentine, Mexican, or
Cuban is unwieldy because of a host of historical, social, political,
cultural, and ideological differences. With reference to the latter,
a number of Latin American writers have commented on what
they see as contrasting views of justice. For one Brazilian writer, a
narrative formula in which the triumph of justice coincides with
the law is "completely irrelevant" in his country.[4] An Argentine
author observes that the law is generally not respected there, but
rather is regarded as an "instrument of repression and oppres-
sion. When we happen to run across a detective story set in *our*
environment," Adolfo Pérez Zelaschi goes on to say, "but whose
technique responds to *your* environment, we immediately reject
it." The author illustrates his point by positing a plot in which the
detective refuses to enter a suspect's house without a search war-
rant, behavior Zelaschi believes would stretch the limits of Argentine credibility in a tale set there.[5] The Mexican critic Carlos
Monsiváis goes so far as to state categorically that detective liter-

ature is incompatible with Latin America because "we have no faith in justice."[6]

It would be as inaccurate to conclude that Latin Americans do not believe in justice as it would to insist that justice is served in the United States and Europe as regularly as it is in mystery and crime fiction from those places. A finer distinction needs to be made between the ideological premises of the whodunit and the hard-boiled formulas, and those of Latin American works which go beyond imitation of their foreign models. The authors of stories such as those in this anthology use the genre to depict and critically examine social, political, and cultural systems and patterns which are sometimes unjust, arbitrary, and violent. The search for truth and justice frequently fails. It is precisely because solutions are often not reached, puzzles are left scattered on the table, and killers are on the loose that these works can become more meaningful. "When detective fiction crosses the border, it seems to become more sophisticated, not in terms of craftsmanship . . . , but rather because it moves toward a more profound text, in a theoretical and ideological sense," Rivera concludes.[7] Pulling against the tide instead of flowing predictably toward the last soothing page that harbors all the answers, the Latin American tale offers no guarantees. Its oft-defeated, diverted, or subverted efforts to seek truth and justice generally occur outside the system, in the margins, without the benefit of a Chandlerian vision of bygone, chivalrous days or a Spillane's evangelical primitivism to sustain the quest. Instead of closure—that pair of handcuffs clapped around the wrists of the culprit—there is disclosure. The reader whose only aim is to suspend time and cares for a couple of hours will likely not be satisfied with these stories. Here we are meant to pause as well as puzzle, and, at the end, to reconsider as well as reconstruct the story of a crime.

Julio Cortázar once wrote a story called "Continuidad de los parques" ["Continuity of Parks"] (1964) about a man sitting in a green velvet armchair reading a suspense novel of crime and betrayal in which the murderer approaches little by little until finally he stands, knife raised, behind the chair of his victim who sits in a green velvet armchair reading a suspense novel. . . . The "continuity" of Cortázar's story, that is to say, the way one level of fiction steps off the page into another level, implies the breakdown of conventional perspective of what is real and what is fiction, what is true and what is false. Similarly, in "The Crazy Woman and the Story of the Crime" (1975), Ricardo Piglia's detective Emilio Renzi opens official "facts" to interpretation. At the end of this murder mystery, the narrative crosses the same boundary as in Cortázar's story. The lens through which we view the fictional landscape suddenly shifts focus and our assumptions are turned inside out. What seemed marginal is now the substance of the tale. We turn the page and feel the knife.

Piglia's use of the genre to comment on institutionalized violence and repression is typical of Argentine crime fiction of the 1970s. The genre has been used as a vehicle for social criticism, however, since the first Latin American works appeared in Argentina in the late nineteenth century.[8] Among the earliest detective literature written there is Eduardo Ladislao Holmberg's "La bolsa de huesos" [The sack of bones] (1896), which denounces rigid, doctrinaire approaches to criminal investigation and prosecution. Many of Leonardo Castellani's Padre Metri stories from the 1930s through the 1950s are radical attacks on the institutions of church and state in Argentina. Rodolfo Walsh integrates crime fiction techniques and documentary narrative in *Operación masacre* [*Operation Massacre*] (1957) about a case of human rights violations. It is in the 1970s, however, that social criticism becomes the central concern for a group of Argentine authors who adapt the North American hard-boiled formulas to address contemporary issues. Besides Piglia, such writers as Juan Carlos Martini, José Pablo Feinmann, Osvaldo Soriano, and Alberto Laiseca produce works that are memorable for their tense, searching, often elliptical indictments of a violent, repressive society. The casting off of real world logic is characteristic of works of this period, and has an important precedent in Argentine detective fiction. Jorge Luis Borges' masterpiece "La muerte y la brújula" ["Death and the Compass"] (1942) introduces a metaphysical dimension to the classic puzzle formula, undermining its symmetry to reveal an unpredictable reality ruled by paradox and uncertainty. Piglia invokes Borges' vision, but in response to Argentine social realities of the 1970s, uses it to suggest a specific image of the menace of institutionalized violence. In "The Crazy Woman and the Story of the Crime," Piglia pays homage to Borges, and also to the classic whodunit with its cult of reason and erudition as the reader will notice particularly in the second half of the story. Piglia also tips his hat to the great works of the hard-boiled school, especially those of Raymond Chandler. In the first part of Piglia's story, the care with which the author describes places and people to evoke a social reality characterized by impersonality and estrangement is reminiscent of Chandler's vision and his attention to language.

In Eduardo Goligorsky's story, also from Argentina, the psychosis of violence is masked by an appearance of normality. "Hierarchy" (1975) presents a vision of encompassing society by describing an underworld social order with its lower, middle, and upper classes of murderers. The first works the streets while the last operates from corporate headquarters. The social-climber Abáscal, representative of the middle class, envisions his ascent as a series of acquisitions on a grander and grander scale—bigger houses, faster cars, more expensive and sophisticated weapons, and finally, one day, death by an instrument worthy of his social status. The subordination of the individual to the system and individuals' consequent interchangeability are the keys to Goligorsky's vision of violent, modern, corporate society.

In "Doctor and Doctoring" (1981), by the Mexican author Luis Arturo Ramos, a crime puzzle is developed to direct our attention to the question of class conflict. Seeking to understand why the scar on the face of a charity patient disturbs him to the point of obsession, Ramos' nameless doctor gradually perceives an unspoken threat—an accusation—in the disfigured surface of his patient's skin. The confrontation with the "other," the "enemy" by virtue of class, is a theme explored in numerous works of Mexican crime fiction, beginning with Antonio Helú's satirical stories of the 1920s. These tales often draw attention to the injustice of social and economic inequality, and express the resentment of the lower classes toward the affluent. Helú's Máximo Roldán (anagram of ladrón, or thief), is a rogue-detective hero who steals, makes fools of the police, and asserts the superior importance of individual over institutional justice.

Arguably the most important detective work from Mexico is Vicente Leñero's novel Los albañiles [The bricklayers] (1964). The novel's setting, a construction site in Mexico City, is a microcosm in which the author explores the anger and resentment bred by a hierarchical system, by the arrangement of men above and below each other on the scaffolding of society. The murder of the nightwatchman at the construction site is apparently the work of a lone killer. Yet the investigation of the crime progressively confirms the suspects, instead of eliminating them, until everyone appears to be guilty. According to one critic, "the whole novel is a metaphor for unequal social relations."[9] Leñero integrates his portrait of class conflict with a mythical vision in this novel, which offers resolution neither to the crime problem nor to a social situation of transformation and disintegration.

The same theme is made transparent in the next story, "Monday's Heads" (1978), by the Brazilian author Ignácio de Loyola Brandão. The dehumanizing effect of class prejudice is illustrated through this tale of an elevator operator in an office building in São Paulo. It is as if one of Chandler's faceless walk-ons—the elevator operators, the small time crooks, the night clerks of rundown hotels, the seedy rooming house widows—were to spit out the accumulation of years of anger. If the spotlight turns only briefly on Chandler's little gray people and then moves on, Brandão chooses to feature his man, following him to work, on his lunch break, on the bus home. By stressing the markers of social class, Brandão attempts to engage readers' sympathies for an individual we are likely to find abhorrent.

Both Brandão's and the next story, Paulo Rangel's "Deposition," were published in a 1978 anthology of Brazilian crime stories, *Chame o ladrão* [Call a thief]. The stories in *Chame o ladrão* explore the conditions of Brazil's marginal population—the homeless, unemployed or underemployed, and disenfranchised sector of society. Rangel's "Deposition" exposes the plight of an abandoned child who turns to crime, as many such children do, in order to survive. It is perhaps of interest to note that the author did not need to invent the story he tells: Rangel witnessed just such a scene. By turning it into a story, he transforms the interrogation of the (innocent? guilty?) child into an interrogation addressed to the (innocent? guilty?) reader.

Social criticism is an important element of Brazilian crime literature from the first work published there, *O Mystério* [The mystery] (1920) through Maria Alice Barroso's acclaimed 1969 novel *Quem matou Pacífico?* [Who killed Pacífico?] about violence practiced with impunity by powerful landowning families, to current works. Parody, satire, and farce are also common in Brazilian crime fiction. In Rubem Fonseca's "Mandrake" (1979), the cynicism that takes for granted corruption on the part of the authorities is relieved by comic interludes including a good-humored parody of hard-boiled detective fiction. The scene in which Fonseca's detective, Mandrake, visits a wealthy client's mansion, complete with a butler and a beautiful woman descending a staircase, is a direct allusion to the opening of Chandler's *The Big Sleep* (1939). Unlike Chandler's Philip Marlowe, however, Mandrake is no knight. If the former, to quote from Chandler's famous essay, is "a man who is not himself mean, who is neither tarnished nor afraid," and who is not "a satyr," Fonseca's protagonist is all of those things.[10] The effect of the environment in which Mandrake operates—an alienated urban society "in the process of destroying itself"—is reflected in the degraded hard-boiled detective, no longer much of a hero.[11]

In "The South Bay Crime" (1980), Glauco Rodrigues Corrêa satirizes provincialism, gently poking fun at the ignorance, xenophobia, petty feuding, meddlesomeness, and overblown sense of self-importance of the citizens of a small Brazilian community. This extremely comical satire has another purpose besides entertainment. Corrêa has voiced the need to be aware of derivative cultural forms and has called for the "brazilianization" of Brazilian crime fiction. In "The South Bay Crime," the author draws attention to the devices and conventions of detective fiction in his mockery of the ingenuous narrator's attempts to write a literary masterpiece. This procedure, which stresses the awkwardness of the narrator's efforts to emulate a foreign form, underlines the alien and alienating nature of the exercise.

The last story in the present anthology is from Cuba and needs to be understood in the context of the experiment in socialist detective fiction that Cuban writers undertook beginning in 1971. The genre was virtually uncultivated by native writers before then, but since has flourished: Cuba is one of the most prolific producers of crime fiction in Latin America. In 1972, authors were encouraged by a competition organized by the Cuban Ministry of Internal Affairs, which set a policy for submissions: "Detective genre works will be of a didactic nature and will further awareness, and prevention, of all antisocial and counterrevolutionary activities."[12] This difficult experiment in transforming a genre that has always been considered a product and reflection of capitalist society has produced some successful texts. The didactic aims of socialist crime fiction, however, tend to limit the genre's possibilities. The predictability of motive and crime (betrayal of the revolution), the obligatory reliability and exemplary conduct of the masses, the necessarily featureless detective who is merely their representative, and the relative facility with which any foe of the revolution is identified, all reduce the opportunities to create suspense and narrative interest.

Some Cuban authors have found ways to exploit conventional devices and strategies while still projecting a socialist point of view. Particularly effective is the use of temporal and geographical settings outside postrevolutionary Cuba. Most of Ignacio Cárdenas Acuña's *Enigma para un domingo* [*Enigma for a Sunday*] (1971) takes place in Havana years before the revolution, when the narrator was a private eye involved in blackmail, robbery, and murder. The framework of the novel leaves no doubts as to how the reader is supposed to interpret that portrait of violence and corruption, but explicit propagandizing is absent from the retrospective portion of the narrative. Similarly, Juan Angel Cardi avoids some of the limitations of the socialist formula by setting the bulk of his novel *El American Way of Death* (1980) in the United States in 1957. Cardi uses humor and satire as well in this novel which shows considerable flexibility in the expression of ideological views.

In this context, Arnaldo Correa's "The Man under the Ceiba Tree" (1982) is an unusual text. While set in postrevolutionary Cuba and overtly following the prescribed formula of denouncing counterrevolutionary activities, the story contains a subtle challenge to the socialist program for the genre. A careful reading reveals that one of Correa's aims is to assert the possibility that there are flaws in the social system (and in the literary form designed to represent that system). Specifically, the detective-protagonist suggests that perhaps the friends and enemies of the revolution are not so easily distinguished after all. This seemingly minor assertion nevertheless represents a significant departure from the vast majority of Cuban detective works.

One of the characteristics of Latin American crime fiction is its great variety. Generally associated with low-brow forms of culture, the genre in fact lends itself to many different purposes and operates at different levels of cultural reception. In Latin America, where mass marketing of crime fiction still relies for the most part on translations, and where the genre is not a manifestation of popular culture, works tend to be less standardized. One's expectations should be adjusted accordingly. The present anthology is meant to give the reader an opportunity to sample first hand some of the latest examples from Latin America of an evolving genre.

Notes

1. Abel Mateo, quoted in Donald A. Yates, "The Argentine Detective Story" (Ph.D. diss., University of Michigan, 1960), 37.
2. Jorge B. Rivera, ed., *El relato policial en la Argentina* (Buenos Aires: EU-DEBA, 1986), 23.
3. Ibid., 30.
4. Moacir Amâncio, ed., *Chame o ladrão: Contos policiais brasileiros* (São Paulo: Edições Populares, 1978), 7.
5. Quoted in Yates, "Argentine Detective Story," 70.
6. Quoted in Vicente Francisco Torres, ed., *El cuento policial mexicano* (Mexico: Diógenes, 1982), 13.
7. Rivera, *El relato policial,* 25.
8. For a detailed history of the development of the genre in Latin America, see Amelia S. Simpson, *Detective Fiction from Latin America* (Rutherford, N.J.: Fairleigh Dickinson Press, 1990).
9. Iris Josefina Ludmer, "Vicente Leñero, *Los albañiles*. Lector y actor," in *Nueva novela lationamericana,* ed. Jorge Lafforgue (Buenos Aires: Paidós, 1979), 1:206.
10. Raymond Chandler, *The Simple Art of Murder* (New York: Ballantine, 1977), 20.
11. Jon M. Tolman, "The Moral Dimension in Rubem Fonseca's Prose," *New World* 1, no. 1 (1986): 67.
12. Francisco Garzón Céspedes, "Prólogo" in Armando Cristóbal Pérez, *La ronda de los rubíes* (Havana: Arte y Literatura, 1973), 8.

New Tales
of Mystery and Crime
from Latin America

The Crazy Woman and the Story of the Crime

RICARDO PIGLIA

Fat, shapeless, melancholy, the nile green worsted suit floating on his body, Almada set forth, putting on an air of secret euphoria to try to defeat a grim and weary mood.

The dark, glistening streets were already growing quiet. Listlessly he followed their gentle descent, holding onto his hat brim when the wind off the river caught his face. The bar girls' first shift was just beginning. There's always someone in the market for a woman, prowling the streets under the city's faded sun, darting furtively across the road to a dance club that spills its tender music out into the dusk. Almada felt lost, afraid, disgusted. With his low spirits the memory of Larry returned: her distant body, soft against the leather bar stool, her knees, apart, her red hair against the blue lights of the *New Deal*. Picturing her in the daytime, the sagging skin, circles under her eyes, swaying under the weak light filtering down from the sky: proud, drunk, indifferent, as if he were a plant or an insect. "To humiliate her just once," he thought. "Break her in two, make her moan and surrender."

On the corner, the *New Deal Club* was a dirty yellow stain, a seedy joint that seemed even shabbier in the early evening mist. Standing in front, a short, thick figure, withdrawn, Almada lit a cigarette and raised his head as if testing the air for Larry's malignant perfume. He felt strong now, capable of anything, capable of going into the club and dragging her out and slapping her around until she obeyed. "I've been wanting out for a long time," he thought all of a sudden. "Set myself up in Panama, Quito, Ecuador." Down the block, he saw a woman asleep in a doorway, wrapped in rags like a dirty bundle. Almada poked at her with his foot.

"Hey you," he said.

The woman sat up, turning her head this way and that as if she were blind.

"What's your name?" he said.

"Who?"

"You. What are you, deaf?"

"Echevarne Angélica Inés," she said stiffly. "Echevarne Angélica Inés, they call me Anahí."

"What are you doing here?"

"Nothing," she said. "Got any spare change?"

"Oh, so that's your game, huh?"

The woman wrapped herself tighter in the old overcoat draped around her like a tunic.

"Okay," he said. "Get down on your knees and kiss my feet. I'll give you this."

"Huh?"

"Here it is, see?" said Almada, waving the bill in his stubby little fingers. "Kneel and it's yours."

"Anahí, I am Anahí. A sinner, a gypsy."

"You heard me," said Almada. "Or are you drunk?"

"Macarena, ay saintly macarena, full of silk," the woman sang, and bent over, kneeling on the rags that covered her, until she sank her face between Almada's legs. He watched her from above, majestic, his little cat's eyes damp and shining.

"Here, take it. The name's Almada," he said, and handed her the bill. "Buy yourself some perfume."

"Sinner. Queen and mother," she said. "Never was there a handsomer man in all the land than Juan Bautista Bairoleto, the horseman."

Through the transom above the door of the club came the faint sounds of someone trying to pick out a tune on the piano. Almada shoved his hands in his pockets and headed toward the music, toward the entrance shielded by curtains the color of blood.

"Macarena, ay saintly macarena," sang the crazy woman. "Full of silk and satin, macarena, ay, full of silk," sang the crazy woman.

Antúnez entered the musty hall of the boarding house at Viamonte and Reconquista, calm, at peace now, grateful for that subtle combination of events that he called destiny, the better to swallow his failure. He had been staying at Larry's for a week.

Before that he would meet her at the *New Deal,* not deliberately, not wanting to admit he went there because of her; afterwards, in bed, they would use each other coldly and efficiently, slowly, perversely. Antúnez would get up after noon and go down to the street, having already forgotten the bitter brightness of the light shining through the blinds. Until finally one day, without warning, she stopped naked in the middle of the room, and, as if she were talking to herself, asked him not to leave. Antúnez started to laugh: "Stay here?" he said. Antúnez, a heavy man, growing old, said "What for?" "What for," he had said, but now he had made up his mind, because at that moment he had begun to be aware of his inexorable decline, of the signs of failure he had chosen to call fate. So there he stayed, with nothing to do but go out on the little iron balcony and look at Viamonte sloping downhill and watch her return, dull, exhausted, wrapped in the early morning mist. He grew used to the way she would enter the room, bringing with her the weariness of men who had bought drinks in exchange for her company, the way she would pull herself together to go and drop the money on the night stand. He also grew accustomed to their pact, to the secret and cherished decision not to talk about money, as if each one knew that this was how she paid for the way he protected her from the sudden fear of dying or going crazy.

"We're about played out, the two of us," he thought, reaching the turn in the hall, and at that moment, before opening the door to the room, he knew she was gone and that it was over. What he didn't imagine was that on the other side he would find sorrow and pity—the signs of death and fear in open drawers and empty closets—in Larry's jars of perfume and powder spilled on the floor: a farewell message or simply good-bye written in rouge on the dresser mirror, like an announcement she might have wanted to make before leaving him.

> He came Almada came to get me he knows all about us he came to the club and he's like some insect or piece of garbage oh my god get away please swear to me save yourself Juan he came looking for me this afternoon he's a rat forget me I'm telling you forget me as if I'd never been part of your life me Larry if you ever loved anybody don't look for me because he'll kill you

Antúnez read her shaking hand, the letters drawn like a net over his face reflected in the glass of the mirror.

2

Emilio Renzi was a linguist but he made his living writing a book column for the newspaper *World News*. To have spent five years at the university specializing in Trubetzkoi's phonology and end up writing half-page reviews on the country's bleak literary scene was no doubt the reason for his melancholy, for that preoccupied and slightly metaphysical cast that made him seem like a character out of a Roberto Arlt book.

The reporter who covered the crime news was sick the afternoon the newspaper heard about Larry's murder. Old Luna decided to send Renzi to cover the story, thinking it would be good for him to get a taste of the world of pimps and cheap whores. They had found the brutally stabbed woman around the corner from the *New Deal;* the only witness to the crime was a half-crazy beggar who gave her name as Angélica Echevarne. When they found her she was cradling the body in her lap as if it were a doll and repeating an incomprehensible story over and over. That same morning, the police detained Juan Antúnez, the man who lived with the bar girl, and the case appeared to be wrapped up.

"See if you can get a story out of it," old Luna told him. "Go on over to headquarters, they'll let the press in at six."

At police headquarters Renzi found only one other reporter, a guy named Rinaldi, who covered the crime beat for *The Daily News.* He was tall and had spongy skin, as if he'd just emerged from the water. They were taken to a little room painted blue that looked like a movie theater: four lamps produced a violent light that was trained on a kind of wooden stage. A proud man covering his face with his hands cuffed together was led out on the stage; the room immediately filled with photographers whose cameras flashed at him from all angles. The man seemed to be floating in a mist and when he lowered his hands he looked at Renzi with mild eyes.

"It wasn't me," he said. "It was the fat man, Almada, but he's got protection upstairs."

Uncomfortable, Renzi felt the man was speaking directly to him, asking for help.

"It's him for sure," said Rinaldi when they took the prisoner away. "I got a nose for it: they all have the same expression on their faces, like a pissed-on cat, they all say it wasn't them, and they talk like they're in a dream."

"It seemed to me he was telling the truth."

"They always seem like they're telling the truth. Here's the crazy lady."

The old woman entered staring at the lights and moved across the stage with small jerking movements, as if she were tied to something. As soon as she began to talk, Renzi switched on the tape recorder.

"I saw I've seen everything as if my whole body were visible inside nerves intestines heart that belongs belonged and will ever belong to Juan Bautista Bairoleto the horseman for his sake I'm telling you go away from here enemy no good or don't you see he wants to skin me and make petticoats lace silk clothes braiding the hair of Anahí the gypsy macarena ay saintly macarena you are dirt, you have no soul and the shine in that hand a flint drank acid I swear if you come near I'll drink acid sinner crazy with envy because I am clean of all evil I am a saint Echevarne Angélica Inés they call me Anahí Hitler was right when he said everyone from Entre Ríos should be killed I am a witch or I am a gypsy and I am the queen that weaves the silk shine in that hand must be covered a flint the shine that made her die why do you remove your veil little mask that saw me or he didn't see me and he talked about that money Mother Mary Mother Mary in the doorway Anahí was a gypsy and was a queen and was a friend of Evita Perón and where is purgatory if she wasn't in Lanús where did they take the virgin with a mask in that machine with a silk veil to cover her face that I took for the white of innocence."

"It's like a Macbeth parody," Rinaldi, the scholar, whispered. "Remember? The tale told by a madman, signifying nothing."

"By an idiot, not a madman," Renzi corrected. "By an idiot. And who said it doesn't mean anything?"

The woman went on talking with her face turned toward the light.

"Why do they call me a traitor know why I'm going to tell you because the handsomest man on earth loved me Juan Bautista Bairoleto horseman with a cloak puffed out by the wind he's a balloon a fat balloon that floats in the yellow light stay away if you don't I'm telling you don't touch me with the sword because in the light is where I saw I've seen everything as if my whole body were visible inside nerves intestines heart that belonged belongs and will ever belong."

"She's starting all over again," Rinaldi said.

"Maybe she's trying to say something."

"Who? That lady? Can't you see she's nuts?" he said, getting up out of the chair. "You coming?"

"No, I'll stay."

"Look, pal, in case you hadn't noticed, she's been repeating the same thing over and over since they picked her up."

"Exactly," said Renzi, changing cassettes. "That's why I want to listen: because she says the same thing every time."

Three hours later Renzi placed on old Luna's surprised desk a literal transcription of the crazy woman's monologue, underlined with different colored pencils and crisscrossed with marks and numbers.

"I have proof that Antúnez didn't kill the woman. It was somebody else, the guy he named, Almada, the fat man."

"Let me get this straight," said Luna, sarcastically. "Antúnez says it was Almada and you believe it."

"No. It's the crazy woman who says so, the crazy lady who's been telling the same story over and over again for ten hours without making sense. But it's precisely because she repeats the same thing that she does make sense. There's a set of rules in linguistics, a code to analyze psychotic language."

"Listen kid," said Luna slowly. "You don't want to waste my time."

"Hold on, let me explain. In a delirium, a psychotic repeats, or, more accurately, is compelled to repeat, certain fixed verbal structures, like a mold, you see, a mold that fills up with words. To analyze that structure, there are thirty-six verbal categories called logical operators. It's like a map, you superimpose them on what the person is saying and you find out there's order to the delirium, that what's repeated are formulas. Whatever isn't part of the order, whatever can't be classified, whatever is left over, the excess, is what's new: that's what the person is trying to say, in spite of the compulsive repetition. So I used the method to analyze the crazy woman's delirium. If you look at it, you'll see she repeats a number of formulas, but there's a series of phrases, of words, that can't be classified, that don't fit into the structure. I went through and separated out those words, and what's left over?" said Renzi, lifting his head to look at Luna. "You want to know what's left over? This sentence: *The fat man was waiting for her in the doorway and he didn't see me and he talked about money and the shine in that hand made her die.* You see?" Renzi concluded triumphantly. "The murderer is the fat man, Almada."

Old Luna looked impressed and bent over the page again.

"You see what I'm saying?" insisted Renzi. "Those are the exact words she says, they're underlined in red, and she puts them in between the words she compulsively repeats, the Bairoleto story, the virgin, the whole delirium. If you look at the different versions, you see the only words that change are the ones she uses to try to say what she saw."

"Hey, that's really amazing. They teach you this in college?"

"Don't give me that."

"I'm not, I'm being serious. So now what are going to do with this stuff? Write your thesis?"

"What do you mean what am I going to do? We'll publish it in the paper."

Old Luna smiled as if he hurt somewhere.

"Now just slow down there, kid. What do you think this is, a linguistics journal?"

"We have to publish it, don't you see? So Antúnez' lawyer can use it to defend him. Don't you see the man's innocent?"

"Look, the guy's screwed, he doesn't even have a lawyer. He's a pimp and he killed her because sooner or later that's what happens to hookers, they're all crazy. I'll admit your little word game is clever, but that's as far as it goes. Give me fifty lines about the girl getting stabbed to death and . . ."

"Listen, Mr. Luna," Renzi cut in. "The guy's going to spend the rest of his life in prison."

"I know. But I've been in this business for thirty years and if there's one thing I've learned it's this: you don't argue with the police. If they say the Virgin Mary killed her, you write the Virgin Mary killed her."

"All right," Renzi said, gathering up his papers. "In that case, I'll send these to the judge."

"Hey, why ruin your life? Over a crazy lady and a pimp? Why get involved?" His face shone with a tenderness, an uncharacteristic serenity. "Look, take the rest of the day off, go to the movies, do whatever you want but stay out of trouble. Go anywhere near the police and you're fired."

Renzi sat down at the typewriter and inserted a blank sheet of paper. Compose a letter of resignation; write to the judge. Outside, the lights of the city were like cracks in the darkness. He lit a cigarette and sat there quietly, thinking about Almada, Larry, hearing the crazy woman talking about Bairoleto. Then he bowed his head and began to type almost without thinking, as if someone were dictating to him:

Fat, shapeless, melancholy, the nile green worsted suit floating on his body, Almada set forth, putting on an air of secret euphoria to try to defeat a grim and weary mood.

Hierarchy

EDUARDO GOLIGORSKY

Abáscal was surprised to discover he had lost him in the shadows of the deserted street. It was already almost dawn, and a few shreds of damp mist clung to the darkened doorways. But there was no reason to worry. He, Abáscal, had yet to let anyone slip through his hands. That sorry fool was not about to be the first. Right. El Cholo appeared again at the corner, where the wind was lifting the mist in a whirling dance. The yellow glow of a streetlight shone down on him.

El Cholo was holding himself rigidly erect, walking along with the stiff posture of a drunk trying not to appear drunk. He wasn't being careful. He felt safe.

Abáscal had started tailing him at eight that evening. First, he watched him go downstairs into the sordid Güemes Gallery, from whose interior there emanated a nasal, droning music. Colorful posters with the exotic stage names of the performers promised a stimulating show. He ought to force himself to go down too, the darkness his accomplice, and watch a monotonous parade of bored females. For Abáscal, the sagging, lined flesh, mercilessly pierced by spotlights, would put a damper on any appetite. As if that weren't enough, a stench of sweat, grease, and moth-eaten upholstery impregnated the rancid air, clinging to clothes and skin alike.

He wondered what El Cholo saw in the place. And the answer came immediately, as soon as the question itself was posed.

El Cholo belonged to a category of humans whose tastes and pleasures he, Abáscal, would never be able to understand. El Cholo lived in Retiro in a boarding house, really a tenement house, sharing a minuscule room with several other men from back home who had recently made the move to the big city. He dressed terribly, even when he had money: a wornout shirt, rag-

31

ged pants and jacket, scuffed and torn loafers. He was nothing more than a small-time crook handy with a knife. Just another knifeman with no ambition, or with a ridiculous idea of ambition. Useful at times, but dangerous now because of what he knew ever since the last job he had performed in an emergency when all the trustworthy and responsible experts, like himself, Abáscal, were out of the country. Because lately, more and more, operations were carried out on an international scale, and travel was the order of the day.

In any case, resorting to El Cholo had been imprudent. With money in his pocket, the bum didn't know how to be discrete, keep his mouth shut. Abáscal had followed him from the underground club to a dive on May 25th Avenue, and then to another, and another, and watched him down all the lousy drinks they served him, and handle the bar girls, and act important by talking about what should never be talked about. He didn't name names, fortunately, nor refer to specific, identifiable incidents, because if he had, Abáscal, who was keeping a sharp ear from the next booth, would have had to take care of him right then and there, in front of everybody, however unprofessional and reckless it might have been.

To take such a risk wasn't smart. Besides the organization that had been so much work to put together, it would threaten the double life that he, Abáscal, the strategist, had always protected so zealously. Because he was into other things, he moved in other circles. His models, those whose style he tried to emulate, were found at embassy receptions, at the big casinos, in the salons of statesmen, at business conventions. Above all he was concerned with appearances: well-tailored suits, exclusive restaurants, new and rising starlets, the best liquor, sportscars, first class travel. Why at this very moment, as he prowled down Retiro after El Cholo, he was carrying a ticket for a flight that left in a few hours for Caracas. Far away from El Cholo's body and the suspicions that his elimination might arouse in some circles.

On this point the lawyer had been adamant. Kill and make yourself scarce. The flight number, stamped on the ticket, put a strict time limit on the operation. Too bad that the lawyer, usually so demanding, had committed the egregious error of contracting a rat like El Cholo, in the absence of the real pros. Now, as usual,

Abáscal had to risk his skin to get everybody out of hot water. Although this too would change some day. He was aiming high, very high, in the organization.

Abáscal slipped a hand inside his jacket and reached for the holster strapped over his shoulder and around the armpit. His hand brushed the ticket folder. He smiled. Then his fingers found the grooved butt of the Luger, caressed it almost sensually and closed tightly, squeezing the grip.

There was also a hierarchy of weaponry. A long time ago, he had seen El Cholo's weapon of choice. A homemade knife whose blade was tapered by infinite strokes with a whetstone. Two lengths of twine bound the wooden handle that was polished by use and beginning to crack. Naturally that was the knife El Cholo had used on the last job, leaving a unique, unmistakable signature. One more reason that, right there at the weakest link, the chain that rose to nameless heights must be broken.

The blue steel of Abáscal's pistol, on the other hand, was stamped with the nobility of its lineage. When he took it apart and oiled it, piece by piece, meticulously, he liked to fantasize about the personalities of its previous owners. A bold Prussian junker who had chosen to shoot himself in the head rather than admit defeat outside Leningrad? Or a lieutenant under Field Marshall Rommel, dead in the hot sands of El Alamein? He had bought the Luger, in fact, in a bazaar in Tangiers where peddlars haggled over their booty of steel helmets, swastikas and other trophies carried off from the desert's vast expanses.

Needless to say, his ambitions went beyond the Luger. Abáscal knew there existed a more advanced, more deadly arsenal, whose use was reserved for other levels of the hierarchy, so that it had become a sort of status symbol. In his ascent, which doubtless would be swift, he too would gain access to that legendary arsenal, the exclusive patrimony of the powerful.

Curiously, for Abáscal, the hierarchy had another side to it. It wasn't only a matter of how to kill, but also, in parallel fashion, how to die. He was horrified at the thought that a crude, vulgar weapon like El Cholo's might one day be found sticking in his guts. While the Luger would raise El Cholo a notch, even it wouldn't be enough for him, for Abáscal, when he reached the top. The rules of the game were not unknown and he, a fatalist by

conviction, accepted them: he would not be dying in bed. All he
asked was that, when his turn came, his executioners should
choose a dignified instrument and not bungle the job.

This train of thought was interrupted when his quarry suddenly stopped at the next intersection. Probably El Cholo's in-
stinct, sharpened in the hill country of Orán and in the intrigues
and double crosses of Buenos Aires, had been alerted. A few
overly persistent steps on a deserted street. An intrusive vibration
in the atmosphere. The awareness of danger lying in wait nearby
had helped clear his mind and he spun around in a crouch. The
knife that sliced the mist into lacework suddenly became the
natural extension of the hand that grasped it.

Abáscal was ready with the Luger. He fired from a safe distance, one shot only, and the bullet made a neat hole in El Cholo's
forehead.

Mission completed.

The clacking of typewriters was dimly heard in the office
through a barrier of acoustic isolation. From the tall picture windows the city of ants reached to the horizon. Beyond, where moles
had burrowed their paths, was the tawny yellow strip of the River
Plate. Smog formed a blanket over the city and the water.

The lawyer began by picking up the cable from Caracas that his
secretary had just deposited on the desk, next to a photograph of
a blond woman with delicate, aristocratic features, posing in a
garden next to two equally blond children. He already knew what
the cable would say: "Contract signed." It couldn't be anything
else. The organization functioned like a well-oiled machine. That
was the key to success.

"Contract signed," he confirmed, reading the cable. In other
words, someone—it didn't matter who—had cut away the last link,
the product of an unfortunate operation.

First it had been necessary to turn to El Cholo, a venal, mercen-
ary nobody who endangered the future of the organization.
Then, logically, it had been imperative to silence El Cholo. Now
the circle was closed. "Contract signed" meant that Abáscal had
been met at the airport in Caracas, on the very steps of the plane,
by a projectile from a Browning 30 caliber rifle equipped with a
Leupold M8-100 telescopic sight. A rifle that Abáscal, the lawyer
told himself, would have respected and admired, given his prov-

erbial enthusiasm for the hierarchy of arms. A liquidation at the airport, with precisely that rifle, was, actually, the preferred method of the Caracas affiliate, which traditionally chose the timesaving approach that avoided unforeseen problems.

A necessary loss, the lawyer reflected, dropping the cable on his desk. Abáscal had always been very efficient, but his participation in that case, albeit obligatory, had irrevocably condemned him. The word from above had been final: leave no trace, no loose ends. Although, of course, it was impossible to get rid of absolutely all the loose ends. The lawyer, in the final analysis, was one himself.

He proceeded to pick up the large manila envelope that his secretary had given him along with the cable. It was postmarked New York. The return address belonged to a firm that served as a cover for the organization. The arrival of one of these envelopes customarily marked the beginning of another operation. At the back of his safe was the code used to decipher the instructions.

The lawyer inserted the tip of a letter opener under the flap of the envelope. The blade slid along until it caught briefly on an obstacle, then continued by force of inertia. The lawyer understood that he would not need any help to decipher this message. He was surprised to discover that at this critical moment, he wasn't thinking about his wife and children, but rather about Abáscal and his cult of the hierarchy of arms. Then the explosive charge, activated when the letter opener tripped the detonator wire, transformed the whole floor of the building into a field of rubble.

Doctor and Doctoring

LUIS ARTURO RAMOS

It was the scar crossing his face from forehead to cheek that was interesting. Otherwise he was just a typical, run-of-the-mill case. Maybe more run-of-the-mill than anything else. Too pale for the country sun, he must live in the city; brown eyes, thin, with a strange lilting melody to his voice.

He arrived in the morning and it wasn't even drizzly or raining to make that day different from any other day. They brought him to the emergency room almost dead from gastroenteritis, his stomach half-eaten away by some malignant virus that would be more interesting under the microscope than in that pale, wasted face. Except for the scar.

You asked for his name and address, and then wrote out a medical history on lined hospital paper. You filled in blanks, parentheses, brackets, without looking at the curving ladder of the scar except in memory, or rather, without ever ceasing to look at the memory of it that was inscribed in your mind the first time you saw it. Pink, smooth between the stitches, conspicuous on the surface of the skin, it reminded you of the series of crosses that indicate railways on maps.

He was put on intravenous feeding, given antiemetics, and prescribed rest. You watched as he listened to the instructions with an expression of not understanding, of why go to so much trouble when after all . . . Then you realized that you were the only one he smiled at, as if you were the only one he didn't remember or didn't think he remembered. From his records you learned that Valentín Espinoza ("with a z, not an s") was a frequent patient of charity hospitals and clinics, that he was as used to the scrutiny of doctors and nurses as he was to the strange little pain of needles under the skin, to the slow coming and going of serum in his wornout veins. That's why, in the beginning, you don't understand why he would smile at you, especially since it happens you look more like a musician than anything else, least of all a doctor. Your father wanted you to become a doctor and you did. You wanted to be a sailor, but never a musician. Still, when people first meet you, they immediately picture you with a violin case or ask about private piano lessons for their daughter who's about to turn ten.

Don Valentín Espinoza (you use the title "Don" not sarcastically, which would be inappropriate in an emergency room, but rather to show that he counts for something, the poor guy who's over forty despite those adolescent eyes and malnourished body) gives his medical history without taking his eyes off the nurse with the good legs except to smile at you now and then. You take advantage of the times when he isn't smiling (that is, when he's looking at the nurse) to observe the scar and slowly (as slowly as the other's nonsmile allows) let your retina descend the steps of the stitches one by one. Then, when Don Valentín smiles (that is, when he looks at you), your eyes move away and you busy yourself with sterilized needles, gauze, forceps. The sterilizing equipment.

He was "destined" for room 51, bed F. (The word "destined" becomes a bad joke in this rundown emergency room, rundown not so much because of the budget as because of the bunch of loafers at the medical school and the brothel that the nursing school has become.) Fortunately, or who knows, maybe not, bed F is next to the window that faces the garden with its patches of sandy dirt and where, beyond the sad little benches and the swings rusting from disuse, runs a high railing through which one can see buses going by and women carrying shopping baskets. Beds F and C, facing each other, both have that advantage/disadvantage. And Don Valentín Espinoza was destined for bed F where he would stay during the period necessary for the cheap serum and the insipid food and the antibiotics to do their job and restore him to full civilian life. You say civilian because the hospital patient's uniform sets those who wear it apart, as if to indicate membership in a military organization, a union, or a secret brotherhood. In the meantime, turning to his left, Don Valentín Espinoza will be able to observe the profiles of the other two patients; toward his feet, the head or the feet of the patient in front of him. On the right,

the most attractive option, is the little garden with swings and
battered slides, the street where cars and women pass by . . . In
short, he can take his choice.

You would pay a visit once a day to room 51, bed F, feigning a
clinical concern that allowed you to disguise your personal interest. For some reason, you're fascinated by the scar, as if it were the
synthesis of a whole life pissed away; as if it were the point (or
rather, line) of convergence of the worst fucking luck. But you
pretend not to notice and you ask about the frequency and tex-
ture of his bowel movements. You take his pulse, probe his stomach, and blame the clan of murderers that crouches behind every
taco stand. Don Valentín smiles sweetly and asks for something to
read. Or rather he asks you where he could get something to read.
You are even more intrigued. You feel a tenderness toward the
pale, scarred proletarian with a literary bent . . . But careful, a
letdown at this stage could hurt. First you ask what he prefers:
newspapers (*The Daily News?*); magazines (*Crime Stories? Hit Parade? Wrestling?*); books? Really? . . . Any particular ones . . .? He
asks for *One Hundred Years of Solitude* or *The Autumn of the Patriarch.*
No, naturally, the clinic doesn't have a library, that'll be the day,
but I'll try to get them for you. In fact, I'll bring them from home.
Which do you want to read first? Yes, I'd start with *One Hundred
Years of Solitude,* then you'll see the contrast with the later
novel. . . . No, it's no trouble, none at all. Whatever I can do, you
know that . . . . Of course, I wouldn't offer if . . . no problem at
all.

When you leave you feel happy. You switch your watch to the
other wrist so you won't forget; a letdown now would be a real
bitch. On the way home you decide to buy new copies, give them
to him as a gift; who knows, if I lend him mine, I might catch some
disease. Impossible. Microbiology . . . At any rate I'd better just
buy them.

Before he was halfway through the first book you asked him
about himself. You went to room 51 and saw him looking out the
window, the book lying open next to him on the bed. From José
Arcadio's madness you turned the subject to Don Valentín Espinoza's past, hoping to get the story of the scar out of him. He's
from Puebla, never finished high school, has lived in Mexico City
for a long time. You tell him you used to live in Puebla too, more

or less at the same time. Quite a coincidence, isn't it? . . . Yes, what a small world.

Sometimes you watch him from the door to his room. Don Valentín hardly ever talks to his fellow patients. They seem to be envious of him because he attracts so much attention. None of the other doctors, including you, chats with them or addresses them at all except to ask where it hurts. But it seems Don Valentín isn't interested in being friendly with the other patients. He prefers to stare out the window or read or just lie there thinking like right now. His hair has grown and he has to brush it out of his eyes. He's thinner although his health has clearly improved. His features have sharpened and now that you know he's from Puebla, you understand why he speaks with a lilting melody. You know he's forty-two despite his physical condition and his boyish appearance, and when you watch him, as you do now, while he lies there not looking at anything, he seems about to disappear he's so gray and absent, like those kites that you let go too high and, at first, they fly, but then they break loose and it's sad. That's why the presence of the scar seems more and more strange, like a nine-month pregnant belly on a seven-year-old child. You almost expect pimples and blackheads.

Now Valentín Espinoza can sit in the little patio without getting dizzy. You go visit him there even though it's outside your jurisdiction. He rests from four to six o'clock in the weak afternoon sun. He's finished *One Hundred Years of Solitude* and has begun reading *The Autumn of the Patriarch;* but he doesn't say much. Mostly he makes small talk or reminisces about Puebla. You discover that you might have crossed paths, seen the same movie or gone to the same show, separated only by ignorance of the future. Don Valentín says "if we had the gift of knowing the future we would have become friends long ago" (the confidence with which he says "friends" makes you uncomfortable).

"Imagine," he says. "The two of us in Puebla, thinking: We'll see each other again in fifteen or twenty years; saying: So how's everything, I hope all goes well till then." You both laugh at the idea. "Have you read Borges?" you plan to ask him tomorrow.

Little by little you realize that Don Valentín Espinoza's life intrigues you more and more; you even realize, with some embarrassment, that you have said "life" and not "scar." Still, you don't dare ask him directly. You become aware that Don Valentín is one of those people whose eyes are hard to meet.

Shortly before he's finished reading *The Autumn of the Patriarch* you find you went to almost the same school. You say "almost" because your school was private and you wore blue uniforms, while at Don Valentín's, practically next door, they wore khaki and little military caps. Both of you remember the same guy who sold oranges and you make fun of the little straw hat he wore that everybody snatched at least once. You remember Doña Rafa, the lady who sold tacos, and the bus routes that would take you home in opposite directions. Don Valentín smiles and the scar gets bigger as if it were smiling too. His face stretches like one of those advertising balloons where you can read a slogan when it's blown up.

Don Valentín asks where you used to live and you don't like the idea of telling him because it answers many other questions too. But Don Valentín understands and nods, a little sadly, as if he were saying, "yeah, I figured as much." His straight hair falls over his eyes and he looks younger and you look at the thick scar, the stitches, and imagine some traffic accident a long time ago.

Only recently you started telling your wife about him. Your growing interest needs an outlet and who could be better than the little woman. She listens attentively and is moved that her very own husband the doctor should show so much solidarity with the disadvantaged. The two of you joke about it.

"What's his name again?"

"Valentín Espinoza . . . But I call him Don Valentín."

Your wife is curious about the coincidences, the books he reads; she's slightly ashamed she never finished reading *The Autumn of the Patriarch* and she puts her finger on the spot, or rather, on the scar. She asks you how he got the scar and you say who knows, but it's obviously the result of some accident a long time ago. Nothing to do with drinking and getting into fights. No, you can tell Don Valentín is from a good family, if a poor one. He probably got hit by a bus sometime.

"Well, why don't you ask him?"

A little while later you visit him in the garden. He's sitting on a swing facing the street. He smiles when he sees you coming. "How are you feeling?" you ask. "Okay," he indicates with a wave of the hand. You sit facing the street too, next to him on another swing. The buses make the ground shake; the vibrations travel up the metal frame and down the chains, making you jiggle lightly on the swings.

"The buses used to go by school too. Remember?"

"Yes . . . Of course I do. The whole room would shake like a rickety old horse."

Both of you laugh at the comparison. You are pleased when Don Valentín laughs.

"Yes, like a rickety old horse . . . We used to throw water balloons at the buses," says Don Valentín.

"We'd even throw stones."

You both laugh again.

"I probably saw you some time and you me, but we didn't recognize each other," he says.

"Didn't recognize each other? . . . How could we recognize each other?"

"Well . . . I mean, in a manner of speaking. It seems to me I did see you."

"Me? . . . What makes you think that?"

"I don't know . . . It's just that you seem familiar to me."

"No, what happened is I was the first person you saw when they brought you in half-dead. . . . You came to and saw me and there's your explanation."

"No, I think it was from before . . . I mean after . . . I mean . . . Oh crap, now I'm all mixed up."

You both laugh and rock back and forth on the swings. The scar laughs too and his hair falls slanting across his forehead.

Although now he's outside your jurisdiction (you like that phrase), you look over his medical chart and discover what you already knew from looking at his face. Don Valentín is much improved and they're going to discharge him in three days. They cleaned and fattened him up and now they're going to send him back out in the world and see what happens. You liked him. His manner. Besides, you're both from Puebla. He has good taste in books. You were almost schoolmates, the only difference was a uniform. You remember the fights with the kids at Morelos ("Slum trash"). The stone throwing and name calling ("Colón's for queers"). Kids' stuff; later on it doesn't mean anything, just letting off steam. On the one side poor kids, on the other rich, a few straddling the line between the two; but everybody up to the same thing, just a bunch of kids being kids.

You tell him how you look back on those days. He nods, agrees. "Yeah, kids' stuff." He admits having thrown stones at the Colón windows. "The kind of thing all kids do, you know."

"It's possible we even threw stones at each other some time."

He nods again: "Probably so."

All this reminds you of a movie where a German and an American meet after the war and they realize they were in the same place at the same time, only on different sides. You tell Don Valentín and very seriously, once more, he says yes, it's a similar situation. You menton it to your wife and she frowns and is a little disappointed. "Oh," she says. "I thought it was something different. Not that same old story."

"Kids' stuff," you tell her.

"Well, it's none of my business. But don't you get any ideas and bring him home or anything."

"No way, you think I'm crazy?" You laugh as you've been laughing ever since you saw the scar for the first time.

You find out Mr. Calvo was his teacher too. You realize that the old man gave classes at the other school too without anyone finding out. Who would imagine. He was such an arrogant guy. Don Valentín remembers him fondly: or at least it seems like that because he smiles when he talks about Calvo. Although it could all be a trick of the scar, frequently, with this type of surgery, the muscles are affected and will involuntarily contract. You suddenly realize that Don Valentín could have been smiling all this time without meaning it.

You didn't like old Calvo because he was a communist. The old bastard. I don't know how they let him teach there. Rumour had it he used to give classes at the university.

"I'm sure he told you plenty of stories about us."

Don Valentín shrugs his shoulders as if not wanting to accept a reality that's becoming more and more evident.

"So Mr. Calvo did tell jokes about us."

"Don't blame him," says Don Valentín. "I'm sure he made jokes about us too."

But you don't say that you didn't even know he taught at

Morelos. You hear Don Valentín mumbling something about railroad workers.

"What . . .?"

". . . they put him in jail."

"Who?"

"Mr. Calvo . . . that railroad workers' business . . . the Vallejo
strike."

Buses go past on the street in front and the little patio shakes
and the metal frame of the swing vibrates.

You don't want to tell your wife because she'll say "I told you
so." "Just as well," you lie in bed thinking. The good thing is he'll
be gone soon. And if he asks for a favor or a job or money. It could
easily happen. Sick people identify with the doctor and then they
want you to perform miracles.

You didn't go back to the little patio nor to room 51. But
Valentín caught up with you in the corridor. You pretended not to
see him and got away. But Valentín knew that whole wing of the
building by heart and you ran into him again. In his hands he
held the two books you had given him as a gift.

"They told me I'm leaving day after tomorrow. Would you write
something in the books for me?"

No way out of it. In this kind of situation there's no way out.
Nor were you going to be rude.

You scribbled a few words and handed him the books without
speaking.

"Maybe we can get together and talk in a little bit."

You said "Maybe" and left him standing there.

You were so annoyed you had to tell your wife. "Who would
believe he reads García Márquez."

That night you dreamed about the scar. Your wife put her
finger on the spot again. "You won't be satisfied until you know
how he got it."

On the way to the hospital you worked out your plan for today:
avoid him or pretend nothing happened. At any rate, the scar
continued to intrigue you. You reached down to turn on the radio
and at that very moment the kid stepped down off the curb; you
braked and steered away until you heard the sound of another set
of brakes to your left. The bus didn't hit you but the passengers
gathered around the windows and stared and on the other side

the kid was screaming and his mother was spanking him as she dragged him away.

You remembered the other time. The kids from Morelos running, carrying sticks and shouting and the Ford accelerating all by itself and the crash. Then the faces at the window, the open mouths shouting and spitting, the sticks pounding the car and bashing in the right fender, and that one kid flying up and smashing against the curb and the pool of blood around him as if he were being wrapped in red cloth.

When they found out he hadn't died, they sneaked over to the hospital to see what he looked like. They watched him leave the hospital surrounded by his family; the thin face split by a gauze bandage, the hair slanting down over his forehead. So the scar and all your fascination are explained. You remember the memory: the moment he saw you at the hospital and the way he deceived you so that you would trust him.

Now you know where things stand. You know that Valentín's arrival on a day like any other day (it wasn't even drizzly or raining) was just the beginning of the plan. That the rest—his phony smile, his gentle, pleasant manner, the lilt in his voice— were a way of undermining any resistance. He must have spent a long time waiting and planning and on that rainless day, when Valentín saw you again after so many years, he knew the time had come.

By the time you reach the hospital, you've made up your mind. You will go to him and, without beating around the bush, you will point to the scar and ask for an explanation that will immediately end the pretence. ("What happened to you? Who did it? When?")

He tells you an incredible story. He talks about sabres, horses, masses of people flooding the streets. A story that starts with his being expelled from Morelos and ends only a few months ago. In Sinaloa, he says, the police surrounded the place, broke through the strikers' lines, and burst into the building. They weren't looking for him but he was in the way. A soldier cracked his skull open with a rifle butt. Friends helped him; they ran; he passed out several times. During their flight they left him at a hospital. He remembers the black thread and the needle; the gloved hands working very close to his left eye; the smell of rubber, the doctor's white coat. But that was a long time ago. It was a hospital like this one. This time it wasn't so heroic. This time they found him writhing and vomiting in a hotel room.

You have kept smiling all along, that is, during the whole story. You imagine the cavalry charging, sabres in hand, as if it were Russia. You laugh at the patient's imagination. You see again in your mind the stone-throwing fights in the old street in Puebla, the bandaged eyes of the boy at the hospital seeing you too through the spaces between the members of his family. In the meantime you pat him lightly on the back and Don Valentín smiles and nods his head. "Don't push yourself," you say. "It's not good to think about things too much."

You accompany him to his room while he leans on your arm. "A relapse at this stage . . ." you say and finish the sentence by shaking your head. Tomorrow he will be discharged. You recommend that he rest, get lots of rest. Avoid street vendors' food. You open the door of room 51 and watch him walk slowly toward the bed. "And no politics, okay?" you tell him from the door. Don Valentín lifts his hand and nods. You know he's still weak and won't be any problem.

In bed, staring at the ceiling, you tell your wife everything. She agrees; she makes fun of the other's story too. She hits the mark, without knowing it, making the comparison: "As if this were Russia," she says. You sleep until 3 A.M. when the alarm clock rings. You have coffee in silence. At the door, your wife warns you to be careful.

You drive through the deserted streets, perfumed by the blossoms of the streetlights. At the hospital, the nurse on duty greets you sleepily and you answer with a nod. She sees you go into your cubicle, already removing your jacket to put on the white coat.

When you open door number 51, the blast of hot air is like a mask over your face; fragments of light from the street filter through the cracks between the curtains. A gentle, unanimous sigh comes from the sleeping bodies. A, C, E, G, and H are empty and the rubber-soled shoes help too. You take the pillow from G and gently bring it down. You push until, through the cloth, you feel the laddered scar come alive.

Monday's Heads

IGNÁCIO DE LOYOLA BRANDÃO

The cleaning woman didn't scream. All she felt was a wave of nausea when she saw Mr. Joaquim slumped over his desk. There was no mistaking he was dead.

Mr. Lemos was found in the doorway to his office, curled up as if he had been cold during the night.

Diva was leaning against the PBX at the receptionist's desk. And Morais, whom they didn't discover until eleven o'clock, after the whole building was buzzing with the news, was sitting on the toilet with his pants down. The custodian made two observations before calling the police. First, it was murder. Second, they were committed by one person. All four bodies had been decapitated. Deductions of a custodian.

The discovery of four decapitated bodies on a Monday brought six police cars, numerous detectives, crime reporters and other journalists, and a quantity of onlookers. Impossible to get through the crowd. The building was cordoned off. Nobody went in, nobody left. People in the other offices complained: it was unfair. Their protests were ignored. The custodian was questioned. The building staff was rounded up: custodial workers, elevator operators, electrical and plumbing crew, the president and the vice president of the tenants' council. One detective with a lot of experience noted that the decapitations had been violent. As if there were nonviolent decapitations, remarked one of the crime reporters.

Questions, speculation, more questions. Who really were the victims? What was the connection? A guy from a radio station was telling everyone it was a political crime. Mr. Joaquim, who used to own a big bank in Angola and lived in exile now, had fled Africa and arrived in Brazil with a huge fortune. In two years he had tripled his money. He held stock in insurance and savings and loans, and financed a newspaper for the exile community. Every six months they gave him a banquet. "It's obvious, just find the Portuguese who support the regime," the man was shouting. "Well, if it's so obvious, why don't you go find them," said a police officer with unexpected patience. "You might even be right." But how to tie Mr. Joaquim to Diva, secretary for a public relations firm, good-looking, ex-Miss Telephone Company, twenty-five years old, happy (according to girlfriends) after her engagement party on the Thursday before the crime? And there was no sign of another link, with the boss, for example, or with anyone else. "Well," remarked an older, wise, and skeptical reporter, "innocent people have to die someday too."

"And that's not all," the police officer plodded on. "There's Morais and Lemos. They didn't even know each other, didn't work together. They might have run into each other sometime in the elevator or in the hall. But the custodian is sure Lemos never went up to the eighth floor where Morais worked as director of a shipping firm. And Morais would never have gone down to the fifth, where Lemos sold tiling, ceramics, and quality flooring."

"Let's suppose for a moment," said the reporter for the most important São Paulo newspaper, a conservative daily jealous of its rank as the number-three newspaper in Latin America: "Lemos sold tiles and ceramics. Morais was found dead in the men's room. Now then, bathrooms have tiles. Couldn't there be a clue there, unconsciously provided by the killer?" "There might be, but I'm sure it's too subtle for me," patiently responded the unexpected police officer. "Very scientific, very Freudian," he added, to everyone's consternation. "My own deductions are simple but realistic. Before long I'll catch up with that blood-thirsty sonofabitch."

"Do you have any leads?"

"No, not a one."

"Will the culprit return to the scene of the crime?"

"The culprit is at the scene of the crime."

"What makes you think that?"

"I don't know."

They pulled out drawers. Searched every shelf, closet, nook, and cranny, under the rugs. They snapped photographs from every angle. "I never understood why they take so many photos. What's the point except to give a couple of people jobs and waste money," said the ill-tempered reporter from the conservative daily. They made sketches, drew the positions of the corpses, took notes, tossed around ideas. The depositions of the custodian and the rest of the building staff weren't of any use. No one had seen the four victims go up. Each of the six elevator operators thought Mr. Joaquim, Diva, Morais, and Lemos had taken one of the other elevators. In general, they knew who had arrived and when, but it was impossible to keep track of everyone in the building. Sometimes an operator wouldn't see Lemos for two or three days because he'd use another elevator. The difficult thing was when someone who worked on one floor got on at another. People in a building rarely leave the area where they work. When they do, someone notices.

The custodian had a question: "Where are the heads?"

A general commotion. The detective who seemed to be in charge called his subordinate: "The heads."

"We're looking."

"How did you identify the bodies?"

"Everybody recognized them. Mr. Joaquim's clothes and his being so thin. Diva was at her desk. Lemos's ID. The handkerchief Morais always had in his jacket."

"We need those heads."

The search continued throughout the building. In the stairwell, the trash chutes, incinerators, wastebaskets, safes.

"We're stumped," admitted a tired member of the military police.

"Where do you go from here?" asked the reporter again.

"We leave it alone. Sooner or later we'll get a break. Pick up some guy to take the rap."

"So you give up?"

"What do you want? We don't have the staff, we don't have the budget, we don't have a lab. The city has two hundred thousand full-time thieves. More than forty thousand prison sentences that nobody serves. Everyone's buying a gun. Seven of every ten people who don't have a job end up mugging people for a living. The police get in on the act too because you can't get by on the salary. We're going to work our tails off over four lousy murders? These people had money. They got in trouble. You'll see, it'll turn out it was a mugging, they tried to fight back and got killed. This is small time crime, just some punk."

"Yeah . . . But where are the heads?"

"Let me tell you, pal. I bet they took them. For soup. With the price of meat these days."

The chief detective sent for the custodian and the rest of the building staff. "One of you is the murderer. I don't know why you did it. If I knew why, I'd know who it was."

He looked at everyone, one by one. And everyone looked at him, expressionless and famished. They hadn't even been allowed to eat their bag lunches. "I know it was one of you."

"Are you accusing us?" inquired the custodian, indignant.

"Yes," said the detective.

"I just wanted to know. I bet it'll turn out you're right. And when you find out who, the first thing I'm going to do is fire him."

"You're free to go now. Anyone who doesn't show up for work tomorrow will be arrested automatically. If found, of course."

The elevator operator of car three, the first to the right as one enters the building, heads down Consolação Street, holding a transistor radio to his ear. He's listening to a waltz by Francisco Petrônio and thinking maybe he won't go to church on Sunday: it all depends on what they find out. In a bar he has beer with an egg in it, eats two sausages in onion sauce, and sees that he still has enough money for a plate of chicken swimming in greasy brown gravy.

"Hey man, want to place a bet?" A guy from up north holds out some slips of paper.

"On what?"

"The soccer game. Palmeiras and Santa Cruz."

"I don't like either one."

"I bet you're for Corintiano."

"No. The only one I like is Penha. I don't like any of the big teams. I don't want to make a bet, forget it. I'm going home to bed, after about two hours on the bus."

He swats at the flies on the chicken. They rise up and circle, settle again on the chicken, he swats again, watches them fly around, alert.

"If you could figure out how to get rid of flies, you wouldn't have to do anything the rest of your life. You better believe it, just ask the other waiter, that's what he says."

On display behind the counter were codfish patties, fried sausage and fish, drumsticks, turnovers, grayish shrimp, sausage in tomato sauce, hard-boiled eggs, and a swarm of green and black flies.

"If flies were bad for you, there wouldn't be a frog alive. And I've never seen a frog that wasn't fat and happy."

The elevator operator turns away. He doesn't want to talk. He's worried. The police are looking for the heads. Because of the police, he had to stay two hours past his shift, and he won't be paid overtime. When he gets home, his wife will be asleep, the kids too. Tomorrow morning they'll quarrel, she won't believe there was a crime in the building, that he couldn't get an advance (and even if he'd had the chance to ask, he probably would have been turned down; he already got this month's salary and over half his Christmas bonus). And the plan to steal a notebook from the supermarket didn't work out either. The kid needs a notebook, his teacher says, otherwise he can't come to school anymore, writing on old wrapping paper from the bakery, pieces of brown paper bags. What does his father think school is? During lunch hour, he wandered around the supermarket and managed to grab some notebooks. He didn't know how he was going to hide them under his shirt: lunch time and all the office workers are there, buying cookies, yogurt, chocolate—snacks to stave off hunger during the afternoon. He decided to exchange the notebook for an enormous chocolate bar; he was hungry. Afterward, he discovered the chocolate was bitter. He didn't know if there was something wrong with it or if it was just old. He thought that someone who could calmly pinch a chocolate bar could easily have taken a notebook too. He ended up with a headache. Must be my liver acting up; I'd better take some castor oil.

He gets drowsy on the bus, his head droops, he folds his arms firmly across his body, defending his pockets. He was already robbed once sleeping on the bus. Now he leaves the house with nothing but his documents and bus money. He has worked as an elevator operator for three years and whenever he lies down he feels like he's going up and down. If he told the custodian about the humming in his ears, a humming that never stops, he's afraid he'd be fired. Once he went for four months without a job, he knows what it's like. The humming doesn't really bother him anymore: the worst thing was Mr. Joaquim, always stern, cold as a fish. Never saying hello. Not even giving the floor number. At first

Mr. Joaquim's chauffeur, a smug Italian, would give the order. "Eight."

One day Mr. Joaquim stepped in alone, didn't say anything, stood there at the back of the elevator, directly behind the operator's back. He always detested having people behind him, it made him uncomfortable. Maybe a habit from the neighborhood where he lives. People on the street, especially when they get off the bus at night, walk along turned half-sideways to see if there's anyone behind them. The elevator operator looked at Mr. Joaquim.

"What floor?"

"You some kind of idiot, boy? Eight."

Boy? He was a thirty-year-old man, father of four. Idiot? Idiot? No, he wasn't an idiot, maybe Mr. Joaquim thought so, but he wasn't an idiot. He knew it was eight. He had asked just to say something. What did it cost Mr. Joaquim to say hello? To say good morning, eight, please? Or just good morning. Some people in the elevator even thanked him when they got out. Because they knew the elevator went up and down safely because of him. If not, then what about that time the elevator was on automatic and it got stuck? And the girls almost got hysterical? They had to call the elevator company because nobody knew how to operate it, even with the custodian giving instructions over the telephone. Idiot? What was Mr. Joaquim's problem? Since then, they had never spoken. What's more, when Mr. Joaquim would get on and go around behind him in the elevator, the operator would turn around and stare straight at the cold, unfeeling man who, for his part, appeared to contemplate the ceiling in a bored manner.

Standing up, all day long, on his feet. Before, there had been a little wooden stool. But the tenants' council, at the request of the owners, ordered it removed. It didn't go with the decor of polished chrome. What does decor mean anyway? Nobody told him, but they took the stool away. On his feet, occupying a minimum of space. Squeezed in if the elevator was full. Squashed. So crushed during the rush hour he barely had room to lift his arms and push the buttons for the floors.

He knew everyone in the building. He knew that at 9:15 Mr. Silva would come down from ten. That the dapper Domingues would go up to seven. Valmir to the top. The perfumed Diva, secretary on fourteen, would stand close to him, very close, even if the car was empty. Practically pressing against him. And the stench! She reeked of those drugstore perfumes. That's why everybody was always chasing after her. People from the other floors got on the elevator all day long.

"Fourteen."

"Fourteen."

"Fourteen."

They were going to see Diva. The woman really stank; women weren't made to wear that stuff. They should smell natural, not rub things under their arms, wash their hair with sticky, colored muck. Soapstone and coconut soap, at the very most, are what natural law permits. Isn't that what Reverend Matias says every Sunday? The elevator operator goes up on Sunday mornings too. Very high, though not as high up as God—who can ever reach God? The operator ascends almost to the kingdom of the righteous. He knew all about the kingdom of the righteous. He would keep his eyes closed while Reverend Matias shouted about paradise, angels, reward, peace, obedience, and love your neighbor. Without being able to repeat a single one of the Reverend's phrases, the operator knew in his heart that one day he would find peace, together with his family, his friends.

"Fourteen."

"Fourteen."

"Fourteen."

"Fourteen."

He couldn't stand hearing that floor number. He asked to change elevators. He wanted to work on the elevator bank serving floors 18 to 32. The custodian didn't understand; he said, "I'm afraid it's not possible," and just like that ended the discussion. The operator went on carrying Mr. Joaquim up and down. Diva, who stank more and more. One day, the operator had an attack, his stomach turned over, he nearly vomited. He held it in his mouth with the elevator full: if he let it out he'd be fired. So he kept on running the elevator with that food wanting to burst out. When the last passenger got off, he took the elevator to nineteen, an empty floor, opened his mouth and vomited even more from thinking about what he had held in his mouth. Because of that woman's stench.

"Seven."

"Nine."

"Fifteen."

"Two."

"Four."

Some people would make jokes. "Are we in São Paulo yet?"

"Drop me off at the airport."

"Garage" (everyone knew that his elevator didn't go to the garage).

"Is this the elevator that fell the other day?"

"Yesterday it went right through the floor."

"No, what happened is it tore a hole in the roof and ended up on the moon."

Lemos, on five, used to play a joke the operator hated. If they were alone in the elevator, Lemos would push all the buttons and smile. He wouldn't say anything, he just pushed all the buttons and then smiled. Then he'd say, "How's it going, everything a-okay, Mac? Everything fine?" Mac. Fine. That's all he could say. Mac. Mac. Lemos didn't know his real name. He doubted anybody knew it. Never, in three years, had anyone in the building called him by his name. He didn't have a name there. They probably thought he never even had one. Why didn't anyone ever ask "What's your name?" Why didn't anyone ask how he felt?

Morais, the fat man on eight, used to get on and, laughing, push an imaginary button in the operator's back. As if he weren't there, as if he were a part of the elevator. How could they think that? His skin was dark, a little oily, nothing like that gray chrome. There was no way you could confuse the two. Skin is soft, chrome is hard, it's shiny, it doesn't feel. He complained about Morais to the custodian. "What do you want me to do about it? Talk to Mr. Morais? I can't do that. Don't let it bother you, it's no big deal. He just likes to joke around."

One Sunday, when the elevator operator wasn't wearing his uniform, he ran into Lemos on the street. Lemos was cleaning his teeth with a toothpick and reading the racing form. The operator stood in front of Lemos, then walked all around him. It's impossible he doesn't recognize me just because I'm not in my uniform. Lemos began chewing the toothpick, spitting out little pieces of wood, one of them onto the greasy, blue jacket of the elevator operator. And he, in turn, pressed his missal tight against his face and looked in a glass window, seeing himself reflected. I exist and God sees me. God sees me and I don't care about the rest. I can't care. On the corner, he leaned against a trash can. I wonder if God does see me? I don't know, I really don't.

On Monday, Lemos got on the elevator and didn't pull his stunt (he had lost at the races and didn't want to talk). Nobody joked. Nobody spoke. Nobody jokes with the elevator operator on Mondays. Faces were frowning, withdrawn. What was the point of weekends? These people weren't like him, every Sunday closer to the kingdom of the righteous. No. Everyone came back to work unhappy, sour, with the exception of Diva who stank, stank unbearably. His daily torture was taking this woman up and down.

"Fourteen."

"Thirteen."

"Twelve."

"Ten."

He opened the door, closed the door, opened the door, closed the door, went up, came down, went back up. "No smoking, please." They gave him dirty looks. "Move back, there's room for more." They looked irritated. Does anyone here know my name?

It was easy with Mr. Joaquim. The man was weak. A hard slam against the elevator wall. "What . . .?" The elevator attendant ripped out the telephone and banged it against the head of the Angolan who went limp. Suddenly, the elevator rose, the door to fourteen opened, and Diva, who was waiting, screamed. The elevator attendant grabbed her, hit her on the head with the telephone; she dodged, he punched her in the mouth, she screamed. Saturday. On Saturday there's nobody to hear you scream. Another blow with the telephone. She fell and lay without moving. Was dragged into the elevator. I'll deliver you to the kingdom of the righteous. But you won't get in right away. You have to stay and purify yourselves at the entrance. Then, when all the stench is gone from your body, woman, you may enter. And when Mr. Joaquim learns humility, he too will enter.

The elevator went up and came down. Where was Lemos? And Morais? He had taken the two up. He knocked on the door of the shipping firm, Morais answered. And fell, under the blows. How easy it is to knock down a fat man. Why hadn't he tried before?

They fall without making any noise, like sponge cake. He dragged him inside the elevator.

It was half an hour before Lemos appeared. "Want to push all the buttons?" Lemos looked at him, didn't say anything. A look of disdain, the newspaper tucked under his arm, open to the racing form. The operator opened the door to the elevator. Lemos saw the bodies. He turned, was hit, and fell. Then, right there on the fifth floor, the elevator attendant maneuvered the elevator a little with the door open. He raised it forty centimeters, the maximum, and stopped it, leaving an opening to the shaft below. The bodies were dragged outside and laid on the floor. With the heads inside the shaft. Then the elevator operator started the car and the heads were smoothly lopped off, falling to the bottom. He heard the muffled sound, like bags of garbage thrown down the chute. Then he carried the bodies, each one to its place. Diva at the PBX. What a lot of blood. He had to use a towel from Lemos' washroom. Morais sat in the bathroom, nauseating, his pants down. Mr. Joaquim was placed at his desk, Lemos at his office door. Then the wiping, rubbing, cleaning up.

Still at the bottom of the shaft. When they start to stink, they'll be found. Until then, the elevator operator in car three will go up and come down, push buttons. Huddled in his corner, without anyone saying please, good morning, thank you. A piece of polished chrome, shining.

Deposition

PAULO RANGEL

"How old are you?"
    "Eleven."
"What's your name?"
"José."
"José what?"
"Just José."
"Can you read?"
"A little."
"Write?"
"My name."
"Count?"
"Yes."
"Where did you learn?"
"Here and there."
"Did you go to school?"
"No."
"Who's your father?"
"I don't know."
"And your mother? Where's she?"
"She's around somewhere."
"Do you ever see your mother?"
"Sometimes."
"Where?"
"On the street."
"Where does she live?"
"I don't know."
"Who do you live with?"
"Nobody."
"Where do you sleep?"
"Different places."

"Do you have any relatives?"

"No."

"Aunts, uncles?"

"Some ladies say they're my aunts, but I don't believe it."

"Why don't you believe it?"

"They just use me to beg for money."

"Do you beg for money?"

"Sometimes I do, sometimes I don't."

"Where do they live?"

"I don't know."

"Tell me where one of the ladies lives."

"No."

"How do you get money to eat?"

"Working."

"Where?"

"No regular place."

"What do you do?"

"Wash cars, deliver messages, shine shoes, carry packages."

"Where do you get these jobs?"

"At the market. Stores. The bus station. Taxi stands. School. Wherever there's lots of people. But it's dangerous. There's always somebody around looking for kids to arrest. You have to be sharp."

"Where were you January 13?"

"I don't remember, sir. That's already more than ten days ago."

"Let me help. It was a Sunday. Not last Sunday. The one before. At seven o'clock in the evening. It was unusually cool. Do you remember where you were?"

"I'm trying . . . but I can't remember."

"Were you in Capivari?"

"No way."

"Where were you, then?"

"Anywhere but there."

"Are you familiar with Capivari?"

"Sure. Everybody is. I bet even you are. Aren't you?"

"Do you ever go there?"

"It's a pretty neighborhood. When I'm not working, I like to go out there. But only during the daytime. Don't you ever spend the afternoon in Capivari? Take the family?"

"When was the last time you were there?"

"Last year."

"What month?"

"I don't remember. But it was a while ago."

"What time was it?"

"I don't know what time it was, but it wasn't at night. I'm sure."

"Do you know anyone in Capivari?"

"Yes."

"Where?"

"At the big houses. When I'm in Capivari, they see me and ask if I want a job. I say yes, so they tell me to sweep the front walk or the patio, clean out a toilet. Then they wrap up some leftovers and tell me to go eat it somewhere else."

"Where are these houses where you work?"

"I don't remember."

"Look at this picture. Were you ever in this house?"

"Never."

"Have you ever seen this house?"

"This is the first time."

"This house is on the central square in Capivari. You can't miss it if you've ever been to Capivari."

"It's a pretty house. Next time I go there, I'll look for it."

"Think hard. On January 13, at 7 P.M., were you in the square in Capivari?"

"After you asked the question five times, I thought about it really hard. I'm positive now. No. I wasn't there that day. When I have some money, I take a bus out to the countryside. We usually make money on Sundays. I was out of town. Definitely."

"This man standing here said that he saw you leaving that house. That Sunday. Do you recognize this man?"

"I never saw him before."

"Look carefully. He owns the bakery there on the square. Don't you ever go to the bakery? Buy some bread? Ice cream?"

"You're right. That's him. He's different. At the bakery he always looks like a slob. With his beard grown out. Always yelling at the people that work there. Today he's all fixed up. Wearing a suit. Not yelling at anyone. There he's always shouting: 'Out of here you stinking brat, you'll scare away the customers.' Or else he's flirting with the rich people's maids, when his wife's not around."

"You know I can keep you here in jail."

"Yes, sir, I know. Are you the one who had me picked up?"

"No. It was the chief of police."

"Isn't it illegal to arrest kids?"

"No, it's not illegal. Who told you that?"

"A guy in jail."

"If we had a juvenile detention center here in the city, you would be sent there. Since we don't, you've been put in jail. Are they treating you well?"

"No, sir."

"They're not?"

"No."

"Why?"

"They left me for days without any food. I don't know how I survived. They gave me dirty water to drink. I got real sick."

"Why didn't you ask them to call a doctor?"

"I did."

"Did they call one?"

"No."

"Who did you talk to?"

"One of the guards. I think it was the head guard."

"Do you know his name?"

"It's that one standing at the back of the room."

"Are you hungry? Do you want something to eat?"

"They fed me today. Now I know why. They were bringing me here."

"So, right now, you're not hungry?"

"No. But I hurt all over from being beaten."

"Who hit you?"

"The guards. They all do it. They punch you. Pinch you. Shove you around. They're going to end up killing me. The ones who picked me up, who drive around in a police car, they beat people up too."

"Where did they hit you?"

"All over my body. I know, you're going to ask me to show you where. But the way they beat you there aren't any marks. They use the palm of the hand or the edge. Or pull your hair. What they do to the other prisoners is worse."

"You saw it?"

"I heard it and saw it. They have the parrot's perch: they strip the prisoner and tie his arms to his feet. They stick a pole between his legs and hang the poor guy upside down. They take an electric wire and give him electric shocks. Inside the ears. On his cock. Up his ass. How's anyone going to know? It doesn't leave any marks. They didn't give me shocks because I said I'd tell everyone. They'll end up killing all the prisoners. Everyone's weak. Sick. They have T.B. They're starving. People bring food on visiting day and the police steal it. They sit there eating cake right in front of the prisoners. They say it's because there could be a file or a gun inside the food. And they make the prisoners ask the visitors to bring more food. If the prisoners don't, they get beat up."

"You saw all this in only eight days?"

"Not eight days, sir. I was arrested on the 16th, in the afternoon, and since today's the 25th, it's been 9 days."

"You have such a good memory, but you can't remember what you were doing on Sunday the 13th?"

"No."

"Do you remember where you were arrested?"

"At the bus station."

"What did you have in your hand?"

"A pair of men's pants."

"And in the other hand?"

"A bag."

"What was inside?"

"Clothes."

"Who arrested you?"

"The guards."

"What were you doing?"

"Selling the pants."

"Where did you get the clothes?"

"A man at the bus station asked me if I wanted a job. I said yes. He gave me a bag of clothes to sell. If I sold them, we'd split the money."

"Was the man alone, or was there a girl with him?"

"There . . . no, I don't know. There were a lot of girls around."

"Did you see the man get on the bus?"

"Yes."

"Then the guards arrived?"

"Yes."

"When the guards asked you if someone you know just got on the bus, you said you didn't know anybody on that bus. Why?"

"They asked me that? I don't remember."

"Those clothes you were selling, do you know whose they are? They belong to the owner of the house in Capivari which was robbed by a couple and an eleven-year-old kid, Sunday before last, the 13th of January. Do you know what fingerprints are? They're those little lines on your fingers. And the little lines left inside the house are exactly the same as yours. The couple, who have already been arrested, confessed that they planned it all with you. They pushed you inside the house through an open window. You unlocked the door. They went in and robbed the place. Meanwhile, you stood there eating food out of the refrigerator. Mostly cheese."

"Cheese?"

"Yes. Cheese. Do you like cheese?"

"I like it a lot."

"So you're ready to confess? You're going to tell me what happened?"

"I'm not confessing, no sir. I don't have anything to confess. How can you believe those lies the police made up? The guards are thieves. Torturers. Murderers. Didn't you hear what I just told you? The prisoners aren't the dangerous ones, it's the guards. They made that whole thing up. That's why they got my hand all dirty with black grease. To set me up. They put some white powder on my fingers too, a few days ago. I know they took that powder, with the prints off my fingers, to that house you were talking about. You should go see if that's the powder that was on the yellow glass in the windows at that house. Didn't you say it was yellow?"

Mandrake

RUBEM FONSECA

I was playing white. I had opened with a fianchetto to develop my bishops. Berta was building up her pawns in the center.

This is Mr. Paulo Mendes' office, my voice on the answering machine said, giving the caller thirty seconds to leave a message. The name was Cavalcante Méier. He said it as if there were a hyphen between the two names. They were trying to get him involved in a crime, but—click—the time was up before he could say what he wanted.

Every time we're having a good game a client phones, said Berta. We were drinking Faísca wine.

The guy called back and asked me to call him at once. A number on the south end, Rio de Janeiro. The voice that answered was old, its vocal chords covered with calluses (of the reverent sort). It was the butler. He went to call the master.

If there's a butler, I already know who did it. Berta didn't think I was funny. Besides being addicted to chess, she had to take everything seriously.

I recognized the voice from the answering machine: What I want to talk to you about has to be in person, can I stop by your office?

I'm at home, I explained, giving my address.

The game's up, Bebe (Berta Bronstein), I said, dialing the phone.

Hello, Mr. Medeiros, how's it going?

Medeiros said not bad, but things weren't exactly good either. Medeiros lived and breathed politics. He had been something or other when the military took over and, although his law firm was the largest in the city, he couldn't shake his nostalgia for power. I asked if he knew somebody named Cavalcante Méier.

Everybody knows him.

Not me. I even thought it might be a phony name.

Medeiros explained that the man owned estates in São Paulo and up north, that he exported coffee, sugar, and soya beans, that he was the government-appointed senator from Alagoas, a wealthy man.

Anything else besides owning a lot of land? Skeletons in the closet, shady financial deals, is he a sexual pervert?

You think everyone's a snake, don't you? The Senator is a highly respected public figure, a business leader, an exemplary citizen, beyond reproach.

I reminded him that J. J. Santos, the banker, was beyond reproach too and I had had to save him from the hands of a maniacal transvestite at a Barra motel.

He gave you a Mercedes and this is how you thank him?

He hadn't given me the car. Like a bank, I had extorted fees and interest.

Medeiros, in a mellifluous voice: What's the problem with Cavalcante Méier?

I said I didn't know.

Let's finish the game, said Berta.

You want me to meet the guy at the door naked? I said.

I was getting dressed when the doorbell rang, three times in ten seconds. An impatient man, used to doors that opened quickly.

Cavalcante Méier was slim, elegant, fifty years old. His nose was slightly crooked. His eyes were deep-set, greenish-brown, intense.

I am Rodolfo Cavalcante Méier. Perhaps you've heard of me.

I know who you are. I looked up your record.

My record?

Yes. I saw he was looking at the drink in my hand. Have a glass of Faísca?

No, thank you, he said evasively, wine gives me a headache. Mind if I sit down?

Landowner, exporter, government-appointed senator from Alagoas, services rendered to the revolution, I said.

Irrelevant, he interrupted curtly.

Member of the Rotary Club, I said, snidely.

Just the Country Club.

A leader, a man of means, a patriot.

He looked at me and said firmly, don't play games with me.

I'm not playing games. I'm a patriot too. In a different way. For
example: I have no desire to declare war on Argentina.

I've read your record too, he said, imitating me. Cynical, unscrupulous, competent. Specialist in cases of extorsion and fraud.

His voice sounded like a recording. It reminded me of one of
those laughing boxes where you pull a string and out comes a
sound that isn't either human or animal. Cavalcante Méier had
pulled his own string, and what came out was the voice of a
landowner talking to a sharecropper.

Competent, yes; unscrupulous and cynical, no. Just a man who
lost his innocence, I said.

Another tug on the string. Have you read the papers?

I answered that I never read the papers and he told me that a
young girl had been found dead in Barra, in her car. The story
was in all the papers.

The girl was my, uh, well, connected to me, you see.

Your lover?

Cavalcante Méier swallowed hard. We had broken up. I thought
Marly ought to find someone her own age, get married, have kids.

Neither of us spoke. The phone rang, hello Mandrake. I turned
off the speaker.

Go on.

Our relationship was very discreet, I'd even call it secret. Nobody knew about it. She was found dead on Friday. On Saturday I
received a phone call from a man threatening me, saying I had
killed her and he had proof that we were lovers. Letters. I don't
know what letters he was talking about.

Cavalcante Méier said he hadn't gone to the police because his
political enemies would take advantage of the scandal. Beyond
that, he didn't know anything about the crime. And his only
daughter was getting married that month.

Going to the police would be pointless, both ethically and so-
cially. I want you to find the guy, see what he wants and take care
of it. I'm prepared to pay in order to avoid a scandal.

What's the guy's name?

Márcio, that's the name he gave me. He wants me to meet him at
a place called Gordon's, in Ipanema, tonight at ten. He'll be riding
a motorcycle and wearing a black jacket with "Jesus" printed on
the back.

We agreed that I would meet Márcio and negotiate the price to keep his mouth shut. It could be expensive, or not worth a dime.

I asked who had recommended me.

Mr. Medeiros, he said, getting up. He left without shaking hands, just a nod of the head.

I went looking for the laughing box. After rummaging around in the closet, the desk, numerous drawers, I finally found it in the kitchen. Mrs. Balbina, the maid, adores listening to it.

I took the box to the bedroom, lay down and pulled the string. A convulsive and disturbing chortle, a gagging in the throat, turning purple, like someone with a funnel stuck up his ass and the laughter passing through his body and coming out deadly through the mouth, choking the lungs and brain. That called for a little more Faísca wine. When I was a kid, a man in front of me at the movies had a laughing attack that was so strong he died. Every now and then I think of him.

Why are you listening to that horrible noise? You're crazy, said Berta. Want to finish the game?

Right now I'm going to read the newspapers, I said.

Shit, said Berta, sweeping the chess board and all the pieces to the floor. Impulsive woman.

The newspapers were on the night stand. A young secretary found murdered in her car in Barra. Shot in the head. The victim's jewelry and documents had not been taken. The police had ruled out robbery. The victim usually went to work and returned home early. She seldom went out at night. She didn't have a boyfriend. The neighbors described her as a quiet, nice girl. Her parents said she would go to her room and read when she got home from work. She read a lot, her mother said, and liked poetry and novels, she was a sweet, obedient daughter, without her, life is empty. There were several photos of Marly in the newspapers, tall and thin, long hair. Her eyes looked sad. Or was it only my impression? I'm an incurable romantic.

Eventually I joined Berta for another game. I opened with black, King's pawn. Berta copied my move. I immediately moved my knights. Berta kept copying me, creating symmetrical positions that would lead to victory for whomever was more patient and made fewer mistakes—in other words, Berta. I'm too jumpy. I play chess to get on my own nerves, explode *in camera*, because outside it's dangerous; I can't afford to lose control.

I tried to remember the Capablanca game with Tarrasch, St.

Petersburg, 1914, where the four knights had opened and a terrible trap had been devised, but what trap? I couldn't remember, my mind was on Gordon's and the motorcyclist.

It won't do you any good to give me that victorious look, I said, I have to go.

Now? In the middle of the game? Again? You're a coward, as soon as you know you're about to lose, you take off.

You're right. But besides that, I have to see a client.

Berta raised her arms and lifted her hair up to fasten it. A woman's armpit is a work of art, especially if she's thin and has muscles like Berta. Her armpit also smells great, when it isn't coated with deodorant, of course. A sweet-sour odor that arouses me immediately. She knows this.

I'm going to meet a guy on a motorcycle at Gordon's.

A guy on a motorcycle, huh?

There's a Hitchcock on TV at eleven.

I don't like television and I detest dubbed films, Berta said, testily.

Then stay here and study the Nimzovich opening, it has some good positional maneuvering. I'll be back in a little while.

Berta said she wouldn't wait up, that I showed her neither consideration nor respect.

As soon as I pulled up in front of Gordon's, I saw the guy on the motorcycle. He was a short, strong kid, with dark brown hair. He was arguing, in a swaggering manner, with a girl. Her hair was so black it looked dyed, and her face was very pale, different from the sun-tanned crowd that you usually saw at Gordon's. Maybe her pale face made her hair look darker and her hair made her face look more pale, and her face made her hair . . . while I was playing around with this idea, remembering the Quaker on the box of oatmeal that I used to eat when I was a little kid, the girl sat down on the back of the motorcycle and they took off fast down Visconde de Pirajá. I couldn't follow, my car was blocked. I hopped out, went into Gordon's, sat down at the counter and asked for a coke and a sandwich. I ate slowly. I waited for an hour. They didn't come back.

Berta was in bed, asleep, with the television on.

I called Cavalcante Méier.

The apostle didn't show up, I said. I didn't bother explaining what had happened.

What are you going to do? He was keeping his voice low,

speaking with his lips touching the receiver. My clients always talk like that on the phone. It irritates me.

Nothing. I'm going to bed. We'll talk tomorrow. I hung up.

I kissed Berta softly on the lips. She woke up.

Tell me you love me, said Berta.

When I got up the next morning, I already felt like having some wine. Berta didn't like me drinking so early, but Portuguese wine can't hurt you, no matter what time it is. I switched on the answering machine and there was a message from Cavalcante Méier.

I dialed.

Have you seen the papers, Cavalcante Méier asked.

I just woke up, I lied. What time is it?

Noon. Have you seen the papers? No, of course you haven't. The police say they have a suspect.

They always have a suspect, who's usually innocent.

Since I'm innocent, I could be their suspect, according to that logic. Another thing, Márcio called. He said he's coming to my house this afternoon.

I'll be there. You can introduce me as your private secretary.

How long have you been drinking wine, Berta asked, coming into the living room.

I explained that Churchill used to drink champagne and smoke cigars when he got up, and he won the war.

I read the newspapers, smoking a dark, Suerdieck panatela. There was a lot on Marly's murder, but nothing new. There was nothing about a suspect.

I called Raul. The murder of the girl in Barra. What's the word on that?

Which girl? The one they strangled, the one that got run over, the one with a bullet in her head, the one

Shot in the head.

Marly Moreira, secretary at Cordovil & Méier. My people are on the case.

They say there's a suspect. Do you know anything about that? I'll find out.

Cavalcante Méier lived in Gávea. I stopped the car at the entrance gate and rang the bell. A private security guard came out of the guard house. He had a revolver in his belt and looked like he didn't know how to use it. He opened the gate.

You're Mr. Paulo Mendes? he asked.

Yes.

Go on in.

You ought to ask for an ID.

Startled, he fiddled with his cap and finally asked for my ID. Pseudo-professionals are everywhere these days.

I walked up a tree-lined driveway and along a well-kept lawn. English grass, no doubt. The butler opened the door. He really was old, as I had imagined. His face showed the hatred and his back the hump of many years of licking boots. The reverent voice took my name and asked me to wait.

I paced back and forth in the marble hall. There was a long staircase that led to the second floor. A girl came down the stairs accompanied by a dalmation. The girl had blond hair and was wearing jeans and a tight knit top. I couldn't take my eyes off her. When she reached me, she asked in an impersonal voice: Are you waiting for someone? Blue eyes.

Mr. Cavalcante Méier.

Papa knows you're here? Her eyes went through me as if I were made of glass.

The butler went to tell him.

Without a word, she turned away, opened the door and left, accompanied by the dog.

One day, when I was a teenager, I was walking down the street and I saw a pretty girl and fell head over heels in love. She went by me and we continued walking in opposite directions, me with my head turned, watching her disappear in the distance, agile and noble, *avec sa jambe de statue,* until she vanished into the crowd. Finally, in despair, I turned around, away from my passer-by, and banged my head into a post.

I stood there staring at the door through which the girl had gone, rubbing my hand over the scar that time hasn't erased.

Follow me please, said the butler.

We crossed an enormous room in the middle of which was a large round table, surrounded by velvet chairs. And another room, with armchairs and large paintings on the walls.

Cavalcante Méier was waiting for me in his book-lined office.

Who's the girl with the dog, I asked, the good-looking blond?

That's my daughter Eva. She's getting married on the twenty-third, as I mentioned before.

Calvalcante Méier was dressed elegantly, like the first time. His hair carefully combed, parted on the side, neat as a pin. He looked like Rudolph Valentino in Camille, with Alla Nazimova.

I asked if he had seen the film. No, he hadn't even been born when the film came out. Me neither, but I went to art movie houses a lot.

Does Cordovil & Méier have anything to do with you?

It's my export business.

So the dead girl was your employee?

She was secretary to my Director of International Marketing.

A shadow passed over Cavalcante Méier's face. Few actors know how to make a shadow pass over their faces. Everett Sloane could do it, Bogart couldn't. A grimace isn't the same thing.

The phone rang. Cavalcante Méier picked it up.

I'll take care of it, he said.

I heard the sound of a motorcycle. The noise stopped briefly and then resumed. Cavalcante Méier seemed not to pay attention to the noise. He instructed the butler to show the visitor in immediately.

Márcio the motorcycle kid entered the room, his face wearing the same arrogance that had been apparent at Gordon's. At a closer look, it seemed more like a mask that didn't quite fit.

You said we'd be alone, who's this guy?

My secretary.

This is between you and me, get rid of him.

He stays, said Cavalcante Méier, controlling his anger.

Then I go, said Márcio.

Wait, hold on, let's not make an issue out of this, I can wait outside, I said.

I stepped out quickly into the living room. From the window, I could see Eva sitting on the lawn, the dalmation at her side. The sun filtering through the trees turned her hair even more golden.

The office door opened and Márcio left quickly, without looking at me. I heard the sound of the motorcycle. At that moment, the girl stood up.

Everything's taken care of, said Cavalcante Méier, from the door to his office.

How's that? I asked, without leaving the window. Eva ran across the lawn, followed by the dog, and disappeared out of sight.

We reached an agreement. I won't be needing your services anymore. How much do I owe you?

Who was it who said that the purpose of language is to conceal one's thoughts? I asked, leaving the window.

I don't know and I don't care. How much do I owe you?

Nothing.

I turned away. The butler was in the hall. He looked like someone who had been crouching behind doors, listening in.

I got my car. There was no sign of Eva. The guard opened the gate for me. I asked him if the motorcycle kid had stopped halfway down the drive before going in the house.

He stopped by the pond, to talk to Miss Eva.

The guard was looking over the top of the car. I followed his gaze and saw a pale girl, dark-haired, standing about twenty meters away. She was the girl I had seen on the back of the motorcycle, at Gordon's. When she noticed I was watching, she walked off slowly.

Who's the girl? I asked.

She's the niece, the guard said. Her name was Lili and she lived at her uncle's house.

The telephone in the guardhouse rang. The guard left to answer it. When he returned, he went to open the gate. I drove the car over close to him.

Ever see the motorcycle kid here before?

I wouldn't know, said the guard, turning away. He must have received instructions not to talk to me.

I went home, opened the refrigerator, and took out a bottle of Faísca. A note on the table said: you should have tried the Würtzberg strategy. All you had to do was sacrifice the Queen, but you never do that. I love you. Berta.

I called my partner, Wexler. I'm not coming to the office today.

I know, said Wexler, You're going to drink wine and play chess with the girls. Here I am working hard while you're out getting laid.

I'm on a case for Mr. Medeiros. I told him the whole story.

Nothing's going to come of it, said Wexler.

I called Raul. He had made a luncheon appointment at the Albamar with the detective assigned to the Marly case.

A city cop, I complained.

Homicide is city. The cop's name is Guedes.

Guedes was a young man, prematurely bald, thin, with brown eyes so light they were almost yellow. He ordered a Coca-Cola.

Raul was drinking whiskey. They didn't have Faísca, so I ordered a Casa de Calçada. I prefer an older wine, but every now and then I like an ice-cold young one.

Marly had a gold Rolex on her wrist, a diamond ring and six thousand cruzeiros in her purse, said Guedes.

That helps, said Raul.

It helps, but we're still pretty much in the dark, said Guedes.

The newspapers say you have a suspect.

That's to throw them off the track.

Has the name of her boss, the marketing director at Cordovil & Méier, come up yet in the investigation? I asked.

Artur Rocha. Guedes' wary yellow eyes searched my face.

I saw his name in the paper, I said.

His name hasn't been in the papers. Guedes' eyes were burning a hole through me. I wasn't going to screw around with the guy, he seemed like a decent cop.

I helped the president of the firm, Senator Cavalcante Méier, on a little job.

I took Artur Rocha's deposition myself. He insisted he knew nothing about his secretary's life, said Guedes.

Do you think he was telling the truth?

We've checked him out thoroughly. The girl was killed on Friday, between eight and nine P.M. At eleven, Rocha was in Petrópolis, at some friends' house. He doesn't chase after women. What he really likes, apparently, is to show off his money. He had a horse track built at his house in Petrópolis, and they say he barely knows how to ride. You see what I mean? All the rich guys have tennis courts and pools. He has that plus horses and a track for his friends to use.

If that's what a director makes, imagine the president, said Raul.

He must be a partner, not on salary. A salary's what we get, that is, Raul and I, not you, Mr. . . .

Hey, don't be so formal. Call me Mandrake, I said.

They say you're a rich lawyer, Mr. . . .

I wish.

Mandrake's a genius, said Raul, who had already drunk half a bottle of whiskey. He's a real son-of-a-bitch. He took my wife to bed. Huh, Mandrake, remember that?

It hurts, I said.

I've forgiven you, said Raul. And that bitch, too.

His wife put out for everybody. They were divorced now. Anyway.

On the surface it looks like a crime of passion, said Guedes, not very interested in my exchange with Raul. Artur Rocha isn't capable of falling in love, or of killing for love, or money, or anything else. But I do have the impression he's lying. What do you think?

When I investigate a crime, my own mother's a suspect, said Raul.

Guedes was still looking at me, waiting for an answer.

People kill out of fear, I managed, out of hate, out of jealousy.

Straight out of the book, said Raul.

I know he's lying, said Guedes.

Alone in the car, later on, I said to the rearview mirror, everyone's lying.

The next day the papers no longer featured Marly's murder. How soon we forget, as the poets say. The victims must be replenished, the press is an insatiable necrophile. An announcement on the social page caught my attention: the marriage of Eva Cavalcante Méier and Luís Vieira Souto would not take place that week. Some columnists lamented that the event had been cancelled. One exclaimed: Whatever will happen to the many gifts the ex-future couple has already received from all over Brazil? A truly serious predicament.

I started the car and drove to Estrada da Gávea. I parked a hundred meters from the gate to the house. I put a Jorge Ben cassette in the tape deck and sat there drumming on the dashboard.

The Mercedes came out first. Cavalcante Méier sitting in the back. The driver dressed in navy blue, a white shirt, black tie, black cap on his head. After half an hour, the gates opened again and a Fiat sports car came racing out.

I followed. The car took the turns at high speed, its tires squealing. It wasn't easy to follow. Today's the day I die, I said to myself. Which one of my women will suffer the most? Berta might quit chewing her nails.

The Fiat stopped in Leblon, in front of a small building. A girl jumped out of the car and went through a door on which was written Bernard—Women's Gymnastics. I waited a couple of minutes.

Carpeted waiting rooms, walls covered with Degas reproductions and dance posters. Behind a chrome and glass table, a receptionist with bleached hair, lots of makeup, and a pink uniform. She said hello and asked if I wanted something.

I wanted to enroll my wife in a gymnastics class.

Very well, she said, taking a card.

I scratched my head and explained that I didn't want my wife attending just any class, call me old-fashioned, but that's the way I was.

The receptionist stretched her lips in a wide smile, as only those with a full set of teeth can, and said I'd come to the right place, an academy attended exclusively by ladies and girls of "high society." She put her whole mouth into pronouncing "society." Her fingernails were long, painted a bright red.

What is your wife's name?

Pérola. . . Ah, but, uh, is the instructor a woman? Or a man? . . .

A man, but I didn't need to worry, Bernard was very proper.

I asked to take a look at a class.

Just a peek, said the blond, getting up. She was my height, a long body, small breasts, firm all over.

Do you do gymnastics yourself?

Not me, this is the body God gave me, but Bernard could have, he performs miracles.

She went slinking down the hallway in front of me to a mirrored door which she opened a crack.

The students were exercising to the feverish rythm of music blaring out of several speakers placed on the floor. At a fast pace, they would bend forward, heads down, reach their hands back between their knees, then straighten up, lift their arms, and start all over again.

There were about fifteen women, dressed in different colored leotards, mostly blue, but also red, pink, and green ones. In the middle of the room, with a baton in his hand, was Bernard, also wearing a leotard. He must have been a dancer at one time. He was evidently proud of his firm buttocks.

Knees straight, Pia Azambuja! Tense those buttocks, Ana Maria Nelo! Whack!, a swat on Ana Maria Nelo's buns.

Keep time, Eva Cavalcante Méier. Don't slow down, Renata Albuquerque Lins! Bernard used the students' full names, these were important surnames, those of parents, husbands.

The receptionist closed the door. Did you have a good look?

Does he always hit his students? I asked.

He doesn't do it hard, it doesn't leave a mark or anything. They don't mind. They even like it. Bernard is marvellous. Students arrive full of cellulite, flabby, stooped, awful skin, and when Bernard is through with them, they're beauty queens.

We filled out a registration card for my wife.

Pearl White?

My wife is American. Pearl means Pérola in Portuguese. I don't know what's so great about making jokes nobody gets, but I can't resist.

I paced back and forth in front of the Fiat, playing white, controlling the center K3, Q3, KB4, K4, Q4, QB4, KB5, K5, Q5, QB5, K6, and Q6. Power and sphere of action. Giuoco Piano. Sicilian. Nimzo-Indian.

Eva came out with her hair wet, wearing tight cotton pants, a knit top, arms bare. She was carrying a large bag.

Hello. I planted myself in front of her.

Do I know you? she asked coldly.

From your father's house. He hired me to be his attorney.

And . . .?

But has since dispensed with my services.

Well . . .? She spoke sharply, but she didn't turn away. She wanted to hear what I had to say. Women are curious as cats. (Men are too. Anyway).

Somebody was trying to get him mixed up in the murder of Marly Moreira, the girl who turned up in Barra shot in the head.

So?

A blackmailer named Márcio claims he has documents that could incriminate your father.

Anything else?

He's a police suspect. There's more, but I don't want to talk here.

When the waiter came, she ordered a mineral water. God, Bernard, and strict dieting had created that marvel. I ordered a Faísca. We didn't say anything for a moment.

If my father is in danger, you should talk to him. I don't know what good it does telling me.

Your father dismissed me.

He must have had a reason.

I told her about the conversations I had had with Cavalcante Méier, my visit to Gordon's, about the meeting between her cousin Lili and Márcio the motorcycle kid. Her face remained impassive.

Do you think my father killed the girl? A scornful smile.

I don't know.

My father has a lot of defects, he's weak and vain, and a few worse things, but he's not a murderer. You only have to look at him to know that.

I recalled the faces of the murderers I had known. None of them had a guilty face.

Somebody killed the girl and it wasn't a mugging.

Nor was it my father.

When Márcio, the motorcycle kid, went to see your father, he stopped in the garden to talk to you.

You must be mistaken. I don't know any such person.

I looked closely at her innocent face. I knew that she knew that I knew that she was lying. Eva had a botticelliesque face, not very Brazilian for a bright, sunny day, perhaps more attractive to me as a result. I don't like sun-tanned women. It's unnatural. The skin, hair and eyes are what they are. To use the sun as a cosmetic is stupid.

You're very pretty, I said.

You are an unpleasant person, ugly and ridiculous, she said.

Eva stood up and left, walking the way Bernard had taught her.

I went home and unplugged the answering machine. Berta had gone to her house. My whole life I hardly ever dreamed, or I would forget my dreams. But I always remembered two, always and only those two. In one, I dreamed that I was sleeping and I dreamed a dream that I forgot when I woke up with the sensation that an important revelation was lost. In the other one, I was in bed with a woman and she was touching my body and I felt her sensations as she touched me, as if my body weren't made of flesh and blood. I woke up (from the dream, in reality) and ran my hand over my skin, which felt like it was coated with a layer of cold metal.

I woke up to the sound of the doorbell. Wexler.

What have you been up to? You know who's after you? Pacheco. Are you getting mixed up with the communists now?

Wexler said that early this morning the police had showed up at the office looking for me. Pacheco was famous all over Brazil. He wants you to go see him down at the police station.

I didn't want to go but Wexler persuaded me. Nobody hides from Pacheco, he said.

Wexler went with me. Pacheco didn't keep us waiting long. He was a fat man with a pleasant face that concealed the cruelty for which he had acquired a reputation.

Your activities are being investigated, Pacheco said, in a sleepy voice.

I don't know what I'm doing here. I'm corrupt, but I'm not a subversive. That was another joke.

You're neither one nor the other, Pacheco said in a tired tone, but it wouldn't be hard to prove you're both. He looked at me as if I were a naughty younger brother.

A friend tells me you've been bothering him. Knock it off.

May I ask who your friend is? I bother a lot of people.

You know who it is. Leave him alone, and quit clowning.

Let's go, said Wexler. His father had been killed in the pogrom in the Warsaw ghetto in 1943, right in front of him, an eight-year-old boy. He could read people's faces.

Watch out for that Nazi, Wexler said, outside. What's going on with you, anyway?

I told him about the Cavalcante Méier case. Wexler spit hard on the ground—he never used bad words, but he would spit when he got mad—and grabbed me tightly by the arm.

You're finished with that case. Don't go near it. Those Nazis! He spit again.

I called Berta.

Bebe, open with the Ruy López and I'll beat you in fifteen moves.

Not true. Black is seriously handicapped in that opening when the two players are equal, as in our case. All I wanted was to be with someone who loved me.

You're in great shape, Berta said, when she arrived.

My face is a collage of various faces. It began when I was eighteen; until then, my face had unity and symmetry, I was one and the same. After that, I became many.

I put the bottle of Faísca wine next to the chess board.

We started to play. She opened with the Ruy López, as we had agreed. By the fifteenth move, I was in trouble.

What's happening? Why didn't you use the Steinitz defense and leave the King's file open for the rook? Or the Chigorin defense, developing the Queen's flank? You've got to move against a Ruy López.

Look, Berta, Bertita, Bertonga, Berteta, Bertısima, Berterisima, Bertitita, Bertotona, Bebe.

You're drunk, said Berta.

Yeah.

Let's quit.

I want to hold you, put my head in your lap, feel the heat between your legs. I'm tired, Bebe. Besides which I'm in love with another woman.

What? Pulling a Le Bonheur on me?

It's a mediocre film, I said.

Berta swept the chessboard and pieces to the floor. Impulsive woman. Who is she? I had an abortion for you, I have a right to know.

The daughter of a client.

How old? My age? Or are you going for them younger now? Sixteen? Twelve?

Your age.

Is she prettier than I am?

I don't know. Maybe not. But I'm attracted to her.

Weak, infantile, conceited men! Imbecile, you're an imbecile!

I love you, Bebe, I said, thinking about Eva.

We went to bed, me thinking the whole time about Eva. After we made love, Berta fell asleep on her back. She snored lightly, her mouth open, inert. Whenever I drink a lot, I fall asleep for about half an hour and then wake up with a guilt complex. There was Berta, sleeping the sleep of the dead. To be asleep is to be so vulnerable! Children know that. It's why I don't sleep much, I'm afraid of being defenseless. Berta was snoring. Strange, in such a delicate person. The sun was rising, a fantastic light between red and white. That called for a bottle of Faísca. I finished the wine, took a shower, got dressed and went to the office. The building security guard asked, the bed bugs get you, sir?

I sat down and finished my final report to a client. Wexler

arrived and we started talking about this and that, warming to the conversation and each other.

It must be shit being the son of a Portuguese immigrant, said Wexler.

And the son of a Jew killed in the pogram? I asked.

My father was a professor of Latin, my mother played Bach, Beethoven and Brahms on the piano, your father caught codfish and your mother was a seamstress!

Wexler went to the window and spat.

Bach, Beethoven, Brahms, Belsen and Buchenwald, the five b's, on the piano, I said.

His face took on a look of sorrow, a look that only Jews are capable of wearing.

I'm sorry, I said. His mother had died in Buchenwald, a young woman who looked pretty in her portrait, with her sweet, dark face. I'm sorry.

It was the end of the day and I decided not to go home. I didn't want to deal with Berta, the answering machine, anything, anybody; all I wanted to do was think about Eva. I can get pretty passionate about someone, though it never lasts too long.

A modest hotel on Corrêa Dutra street, in Flamengo. I picked up the key, went to the room, lay down and stared at the ceiling.

There was a lamp, a globe dirty with light, which I turned on and off. The noise from the street mixed with the silence in an opaque and neutral phlegm. Eva. Eva. Cain killed Abel. Somebody's always killing somebody. I spent the night tossing and turning.

In the morning I paid for the room and went to get a haircut and a shave.

The Steinitz defense, I told the barber, isn't all that effective, the rook's movements are limited, it's a strong piece and therefore predictable.

You're absolutely right sir, said the barber, warily.

The Chigorin defense puts the Queen in danger and I never risk the Queen, I went on. Everything's wrong, the national anthem with its stupid lyrics, the positivist flag without any red in it, all flags should have some red, what's the point of the green for the forest and the yellow for gold without some blood in our veins?

Everything's going down the drain, said the barber.

While the barber was talking about the cost of living, I read the newspaper. Márcio Amaral, also known as Márcio da Suzuki, had been found dead in his apartment in Fátima. Shot in the head. In his right hand a Taurus revolver, 38 caliber, with a spent cartridge in the barrel. The police suspected homicide. Márcio da Suzuki was believed to have been involved in narcotics traffic in South Rio.

I'm not interested any more, they can all get fucked, the degenerate Senator and his disinfected daughter, the pale niece, the dead secretary and her chattering parents, the motorcycle kid, Guedes, lightning can strike him, I've had enough.

The barber gave me a nervous look.

Back at the apartment, a note: Where have you been? Are you crazy? Wexler wants to talk to you, it's urgent. I'm at the shop. Call me. I love you. I'm dying to see you. Berta.

I like Berta, but my heart didn't beat any faster when I heard her voice or read her notes. Berta had become the perfect person to marry when I got old and feeble.

I called Berta, made a date to meet her that night. What could I do? I called Wexler.

I thought Pacheco had picked you up, said Wexler. Raul is looking for you, he says it's important.

Raul's telephone rang, rang, rang, and just when I was going to hang up, he answered. I was in the bathroom. Guedes is anxious to talk to you. He said to tell you to come by homicide.

I told Raul about Pacheco's threats. Raul told me to be careful.

Homicide. Guedes showed me in right away.

I'll put the cards on the table, he said. Read this.

The handwriting was rounded, the i's dotted with little circles: Rodolfo, don't think you can treat me this way, like an object that you use and then throw away. I can make a lot of trouble, talk to your wife, make a scene at the office, tell everybody, the newspapers, you don't know what I'm capable of doing. I don't want an apartment, you can't buy me like everybody else. You're the only man in my life, I never had anyone else, never wanted anyone else, don't want anyone else. You've been avoiding me, you're not going to end our relationship that way. I want to see you. Call me, right away. I'm going crazy, I'm nervous, who knows what I might do. Marly.

Well? said Guedes.

Well what?'

You have any ideas?

What ideas could I have?

What did you think of the letter?

Have you done a handwriting analysis yet?

No. But I'm sure it's Marly Moreira's handwriting. Know where the letter was found? With one Márcio Amaral, commonly known as Márcio da Suzuki. Whoever killed Márcio searched the room, probably looking for the letter, but forgot to look in the victim's pocket. That's where the letter was.

An amateur, I said.

Amateur is right. He tried to set it up so it would look like suicide, but without knowing the tricks. There were no powder burns on Márcio's fingers, the trajectory of the bullet shows he was shot from above, lots of mistakes, the killer standing up and the victim sitting. I think I know who the murderer is. Somebody big.

Careful, men like that can buy anybody they want.

Not everybody's for sale, said Guedes. He could have said he was incorruptible, but people who really don't sell out, like him, don't brag about it.

Senator Rodolfo Cavalcante Méier killed Marly, Guedes went on. Somehow, Márcio got hold of the letter and tried to blackmail the senator. In order to cover up the first crime, the senator committed another, killing Márcio.

I was looking at a decent man doing his job with dedication and intelligence. I felt like telling him what I knew, but I couldn't. Cavalcante Méier wasn't even my client, he was a rich, nauseating bourgeois and maybe a lousy murderer too, but even so I couldn't bring myself to squeal on him. My business is to get people out of the hands of the police, I can't turn around and do the opposite.

Well? asked Guedes.

The senator wouldn't have to have committed the murders personally, he could have found someone to do it for him, I said.

We're not in Alagoas, said Guedes.

They have hit men here, too. You can hire one for practically nothing.

But you can't trust them. The police pick them up, work them over and they talk. They're not like the hired guns on the big estates, those guys are protected by the system, said Guedes. Besides, you agreed both crimes are the work of an amateur.

I told him again that I didn't know anything about either crime, that I was just guessing.

Raul said you could help, said Guedes, disappointed, when I said goodbye to him.

I set up the chess board and put a bottle of Faísca in the ice bucket.

I don't want to play chess and I don't want to drink wine, said Berta.

What's wrong, sweetheart, I asked, tired of knowing the answer.

I'm not going to keep seeing you unless you quit seeing that girl.

There's nothing going on between us, how can I quit seeing her if I'm not seeing her in the first place?

You have a thing for her, that's what's going on. I want you to stop having a thing for her. You told me one time that you only go for people who go for you, that you only go for people you go for. I want you to want me and only me. Otherwise, good-bye, no more chess, no more jumping into bed anytime you feel like it, no more drinking sprees. I hate wine, you cretin, I only drink because of you. I hate it, I hate it, I hate it.

And chess?

Chess I like, said Berta, wiping away her tears. Instead of being the protagonist of her own life, Berta was the protagonist of mine.

I promised to try to forget Eva. I let Berta win, using the Blumenfeld countergambit. To be honest, she would have won anyway, all I was thinking about was who could have put Marly Moreira's letter in Márcio da Suzuki's hands. P-Q4, C-KB3. Cavalcante Méier surely would have kept the letter in a safe place. C-KB3, P-K3. Why didn't he destroy it? Maybe he never got it, someone intercepted it. P-B4, P-B4. In that case, it would have to be somebody in the house, if the letter was sent there; it could have been sent to the office. My guess was the house. The butler? I laughed. P-Q5, P-QR4. You're laughing, are you? said Berta, just you wait. PXRP, BPXP, now Berta was laughing. Someone he trusts, maybe his wife, whom I've never seen, or daughter or the niece. Like Raul said, you have to suspect your own mother. PXP, P-Q4. Checkmate! said Berta.

Baby, you could beat Alekhine tonight, I said.

You just played badly, said Berta.

I was ready to forget Eva, as promised, but when I got to

Cavalcante Méier's house, Eva opened the door and my enthusiasm returned. I had gone to his office first and they told me the senator was at home, indisposed. I took along a newspaper with some articles on Marly Moreira's death. The story was back on the front page. The investigation had established that Márcio da Suzuki had been killed by the same gun that murdered Marly. Guedes had given an interview in which he said that an important figure was involved and that the police were ready to arrest him, at any cost. There was talk about narcotics traffic as well.

I want to talk to your father.

He can't see anyone.

It's in his own interest. Tell him the police have the letter. Just tell him that.

She looked at me with her impassive doll's face, her healthy, porcelain skin, pink cheeks, red lips, radiant blue eyes, a violent blossoming in the flower of youth. She was like a color slide projected on air.

He can't see anyone, Eva repeated.

Look sweetheart, your father is in trouble and I want to help him. Go on up and tell him the police have the letter.

Cavalcante Méier received me in a short bathrobe made of red velvet. His hair had been carefully oiled and combed, recently.

The police have the letter, I said. They know it was addressed to a Rodolfo and they think that Rodolfo is you. Fortunately, the envelope wasn't found and they can't prove anything.

I tore up the envelope, he said, I don't know why I didn't tear up the letter too. I put it in the drawer of the night stand in my room.

A banker's vice, keeping documents, I thought.

I didn't kill Marly. I haven't the slightest idea who did.

I don't know if I believe that. I think it was you.

Prove it.

He was like Jack Palance, Wilson the gunman, pulling on his black gloves and saying prove it to Elisha Cook, Jr., before drawing his Colt in a flash and blasting him in the chest, knocking him face down in the mud, in the ruts of the wagon wheels.

There are lots of Rodolfos in the world. I can prove that I never saw the girl in my life. You know where I was when it happened? Having lunch with the Governor. He'll confirm that. What's eating you is you're envious. You can't stand anybody that actually makes it, can you, anybody that doesn't end up chasing ambulances?

I don't hate anyone. But I despise degenerates like you.

So why did you come here? For money.

No, for your daughter.

Cavalcante Méier raised his hand to hit me. I caught it as he swung. His arm was weak. I pushed it away from me, that scum, royal parasitic exploiter, sybarite.

Raul was waiting for me at his office.

Guedes was taken off the Marly Moreira case and put on a desk job at the police chief's as of today. He gave an unofficial interview. They think he's trying to get promoted. He's being transferred to the Bangu police station. His mouth is shut for good.

Guedes wasn't looking for a promotion. He believed Cavalcante Méier was guilty and he wanted to get everything out in the open before they could cover it up. A believer in the press and in public opinion, naive, but often the type of person who makes the impossible come true.

How's it going, asked Wexler.

Ah, Leon, I'm in love!

You're always in love. Berta's a good girl.

It's somebody else this time. Senator Cavalcante Méier's daughter.

You want to screw every woman in the world, Wexler said, reproachfully.

You're right.

It was true, I had the soul of a sultan from a thousand and one nights; when I was a kid, I'd fall in love and be up all night teary-eyed and lovesick, at least once a month. When I was a teenager, I made a pledge to devote my life to screwing women. I screw my friends' daughters, my friends' wives, women I know and women I just met, I screw everyone. The only one I never screwed was my mother.

There's a girl in the waiting room, wanting to talk to you, said Miss Gertrudes, my secretary. Miss Gertrudes was getting uglier every day. Now she was growing a hump and a mustache. I had the impression she was squinting at me, wall-eyed. A saint. Well, on second thought, maybe not.

Eva, in the waiting room. We each tried to read each other's eyes.

Do you play chess? I asked.

No. Bridge.

Will you teach me? I asked.

Sure.

I had to control myself not to go flying around the room like a crazed beetle.

My father didn't do it, I know he didn't.

I love you, I said. I knew it the first time I saw you.

Her eyes burned like a torch.

I felt something that day, too.

We were holding hands when Wexler came in.

Raul just got here. I told him you were busy. Do you want to talk to him?

It must be about the Marly case. I'll talk to him. You wait here, I said to Eva.

I was at the door when Eva said: Save my father.

I went back over to her.

If I'm going to do that, you're going to have to help me.

How?

Start telling me the truth.

I won't lie anymore.

What did you and Márcio da Suzuki talk about at your house? How did you know him?

Márcio sold cocaine to my cousin Lili. But six months ago, more or less, she quit doing coke. That day, I asked Márcio if Lili had started snorting again and Márcio said no. I was afraid he was bringing her drugs again.

Where did Lili get the money to buy coke?

Papa gives Lili everything she wants. She's the daughter of his brother, who died when Lili was a child. Her mother didn't want to have anything to do with her. The mother remarried and Lili came to live with us when she was eight.

Why do you say you know your father didn't kill Marly or Márcio?

My father isn't capable of killing anyone.

Then it's just a feeling?

Yes, she said, lowering her eyes.

Raul was in Wexler's office, pacing back and forth.

Guedes says he's going to accuse the senator of murder and he doesn't care what happens after that.

Guedes is out of his mind, I said. We have to stop him.

Raul and I went to look for Guedes. Eva went home. I promised to call her later.

Guedes was at the Oswaldo Eboli Institute, talking to a technician friend. He was preparing the documentation to give the newspapers.

Cavalcante Méier didn't do it, I said.

Just two days ago you didn't know anything about the case, now you come and tell me you know all about it.

I told him part of what I knew.

If Cavalcante Méier didn't do it, then who did?

I don't know. Maybe drug dealers.

I went over every detail of Marly Moreira's life, there's no way she was involved with drugs. And the two were killed by the same person. Your reasoning is full of holes.

I tried to defend my point of view. I mentioned Cavalcante Méier's alibi. After all, you can't ignore the testimony of the Governor.

They're all corrupt. You'll see, when the Governor leaves office, he'll be Cavalcante Méier's business partner.

Guedes, you're looking for big trouble.

That doesn't matter. What can I lose? My job? I'm already sick of it.

Accusing an innocent person is slander, it's a crime.

He's guilty. I have proof. Guedes' eyes shone with integrity, honesty, justice and rectitude. Did you know that Senator Cavalcante Méier has a registered Taurus 38 revolver? The same caliber bullets as the ones used on Marly and Márcio?

Plenty of people keep a 38 in the house. When are you going to make the announcement? I asked.

Tomorrow at ten.

It was dusk when I got to the Gávea house.

What happened, what's wrong? asked Eva.

Where's your father?

In his room. He's not feeling well.

I need to talk to him, it's important.

I was surprised at Cavalcante Méier's appearance. He hadn't combed his hair or shaved, and his eyes were red as if he were drunk or had been crying. A look in his eyes like that of Jannings, Professor Rath, in *The Blue Angel,* fighting back his shame, surprised at the world's incomprehension. With Cavalcante Méier was Lili, her face paler than ever, the skin looking like it was painted with whitewash. She was holding a purse. A black dress emphasized her phantasmagoric beauty.

It was me, said Cavalcante Méier.

Papa! exclaimed Eva.

Cavalcante Méier's words didn't ring true. I've seen a lot of movies and a lot of bad acting.

It was me, I swear it was me. Tell your police friend they can come pick me up. Now get out of my house!

He stepped forward like he was going to take a swing at me. Eva held him back.

Go away, please, just go away, begged Eva.

Lili followed me out. She stopped by the car.

Will you take me with you?

Sure.

Lili got in the car. I drove slowly down the drive in the shadow of the trees and turned into the road.

He's lying, I said. He must be protecting someone. Maybe Eva.

Lili began to tremble all over, but she didn't make a sound. When we went by a streetlight, I saw that her face was wet with tears.

He didn't do it. It wasn't Eva either, said Lili in a voice so low I could barely make out the words.

So that was it. Now I knew the truth, and what good did it do me? Is there really such a thing as innocence, or guilt?

I'm listening, go ahead, I said.

Two years ago I realized I loved Rodolfo, but not like an uncle, or a father, which was what he had been to me up to then, but like a lover.

I didn't say anything. I can tell when someone starts to unload heart and soul.

We've been lovers for six months. He's everything to me and I'm everything to him.

Is that why you killed Marly?

Yes.

Did he know?

No. I told him today. He tried to protect me. He loves me, as much as I love him.

Her face in the dark car was like a florescent statue illuminated by a black light.

I can tell you what happened.

Go ahead.

Uncle told me he was having problems with a girl who worked at one of his companies and with whom he'd had an affair. She was threatening to make a scandal, to tell my aunt about it. My aunt is a very sick woman, she's like a mother to me.

I'd never seen her. Rich families have hidden faces, secrets that are inviolable, dark webs of complicity.

She never leaves her room, there's a nurse with her twenty-four hours a day, she could die any time.

Go on.

Uncle got the letter, I think it was on a Monday. Every night, around eleven, I would go to his room and then leave in the early morning, before the servants got up.

Did Eva know?

She knew.

Go on, I said.

Uncle Rodolfo was very nervous that day. He showed me the letter and told me Marly was crazy, that the scandal would kill Aunt Nora and ruin him politically. Uncle Rodolfo is a good man, he deserves better than that.

Go on, I said.

Uncle Rodolfo showed me the letter from Marly and I saw him put it in the drawer of his night stand. The next day I took the letter, found out who the woman was and called her. I told her who I was and said I had a message from Uncle Rodolfo. We arranged to meet after work. I picked a secluded place where I go swimming sometimes. When she arrived, she acted arrogant. She told me to tell Uncle Rodolfo not to take her lightly. When the old lady dies, she threatened, that lousy son-of-a-bitch's going to have to marry me. I had Uncle Rodolfo's gun in my purse. I shot her. She fell forward with a groan. I ran to the car and went looking for Márcio to get some coke. I did some coke at his house, the first time in more than six months. I was desperate. I fell asleep and Márcio must have gone through my purse and taken the letter. When Uncle Rodolfo told me you were going to meet Márcio at Gordon's, I got there first so you wouldn't talk to him. I told him Uncle Rodolfo had called the police and they were going to arrest him.

Stop calling him uncle, please.

I've always called him that, I'm not going to change now. Márcio was angry and the next day he went to see Uncle Rodolfo. You saw what happened, you know the rest.

Not everything.

I met Márcio in the garden when he left. He told me Uncle Rodolfo was going to pay, but Márcio wasn't going to give him the letter back. I set up a time to buy some cocaine, I'd made up my mind to get rid of him. Márcio was sitting in an armchair, watching TV, loaded on coke, downers and whiskey. I went over to him and shot him in the head. I didn't feel anything, just nausea, as if he were a cockroach.

You didn't find the letter. It was in Márcio's pocket.

I looked everywhere, but I didn't look there, I couldn't bring myself to touch him, said Lili.

And the money?

It was in a briefcase. I took it home. It's in the closet in my room.

I stopped the car. She was gripping her purse with trembling hands.

Give me that, I said.

No! she answered, pressing the purse to her chest.

I twisted the purse from her hands. Inside was the Taurus, two-inch barrel, mother-of-pearl grip. Her eyes were a bottomless abyss.

Let me have the gun, Lili asked.

I shook my head.

Then take me back to Uncle Rodolfo.

I have to find Guedes. Take a taxi. It'd be a good idea to get a lawyer, too.

It's all over, isn't it.

Unfortunately. For all of us, I answered.

I put her in a taxi and went to look for Guedes. I thought about Eva. Farewell my lovely, a long goodbye. The big sleep. I was a body with no one inside, my hands on the wheel seemed like somebody else's.

The South Bay Crime

GLAUCO RODRIGUES CORRÊA

Dramatic Statement by the Murderer to the Capital City Press

"I want to be lynched by the good people of Santo Anastácio do Roçado. I'm ruined. There's no hope left for me. You can set me down in the main square and turn me over to the mob. All I want now is to die."

Brief Description of Santo Anastácio do Roçado, Setting of the Events

Santo Anastácio do Roçado is a small town about twenty kilometers from the capital. A quiet, provincial backwater with certain trappings of civilization: color TV reception, telephone (direct dial long distance), plumbing, electric light, gas and sewer services. Sorry, no sewers: cesspools, a few septic tanks. By sewers, what I mean is various informal hookups to the water drains that run into the bay. The old folks say the town used to be important in state politics. Long Street, which runs through the center of town, begins back at the county line and ends at the entrance ramp to the highway. In what they call the downtown area, there's the square—Town Hall Square—with the new two-story courthouse where the City Council has its meetings too. The courthouse faces the plaza, and behind, on South Bay, is a stone jetty where there used to be a warehouse that boats running to and from the capital would use. Around the plaza, which is shaped like a "U" with the top opening on the square, there's the state tax collector's office, the police station, the movie theater, the telegraph and post office (telegrams are sent by telephone), the drugstore, the Central Cafe and Bar (headquarters for local news and information), and the church, which sits at the bottom of the U. From there, streets lined with a few houses and the cemetery climb straight up the hill. Before you get to the top, on the left, is a clinic for mental patients. It opened a few months ago in the house that used to belong to Dr. Eugênio, who was elected to Congress and lives in Brasília now. His old house is on a shady, dead-end street. Leading off the plaza are a half dozen paved streets. People with office jobs and businesses in the capital live there. Some of the houses have been fixed up or remodeled, and others are in various nondescript styles of modern architecture, almost all one story with garages and surrounded by gardens and lawns. Beyond are the dirt streets with old houses or wooden ones, car repair shops, the gas station, and little stores, all the way to the highway. Across the highway is the county road that leads to the small towns of the hinterland.

My Personal Opinion about the Killer's Statement

I don't believe a word of it. It sounded like a lot of baloney to me. Trying to act like he was sorry he did it, like the public just wanted to get its hands on someone. Nothing more than theatrics. With all the reporters and photographers and TV cameras there, and the crowd watching him, he just wanted to be in the spotlight, be a celebrity. I doubt he gave a second thought to being punished, much less wanted to die. I really doubt it.

How I Know All about It and Why I'm Writing This Story

I followed the case from beginning to end. Not only me but lots of people in both Santo Anastácio and the capital did. I followed it closely, though, living through it all in my mind, because I saw it as my big chance to try my hand at writing a novel. I always liked to write. At school I was good at it. I was always writing short stories. A couple got published in the local newspaper. I entered three in contests, though I never won. But I didn't give up. I thought, one day I'll make it. Why not? I'm still young. I've still got lots of time.

I don't plan on kicking the bucket anytime soon. So, when the case came up, I saw my big chance. That's why I'm writing this story. And like I said, I followed the whole thing real closely. Things were pretty slow in Santo Anastácio. My job was easy, nothing much going on, just endless routine.

I moved here when I got the post office job two years ago. After I flunked the college entrance exams twice, I took the post office test in the capital. Like everybody else, I wanted to go to medical school. That was my plan when I left home, but it didn't work out. I decided I couldn't go on living at home. The answer was to take the postal service test and I did fairly well. The opening closest to the city was in Santo Anastácio do Roçado. I jumped at the chance. The office has two rooms and a little bathroom. The back room was practically empty, only a shelf where they kept the old files, a broken scale, and the remains of the old telegraph machine. I decided to save money and move in there. And it turned out fine. Pretty soon I knew everybody and their business in that town. And don't think I had to steam open the mail to find out! No siree. All I did was join the local news network down at the Central Cafe and Bar. I started spending all my time there, at least in the evenings. I quit studying. I used to do some reading and writing, but I could do that during work. At night I'd get together with the town's intelligence-gathering experts, who, to put it plainly, were everyone who lived inside the city limits—but the most important ones were the owner of the Central Cafe and Bar and the pharmacist, who owns the drugstore in town. And me, since I was soon welcomed into the fold.

A Meeting Relevant to the Plot

In my two years in Santo Anastácio, I only left town a few times. When I did, it was to go to the capital, specifically to Barreiros. I admit the only reason I didn't go there more often was that I couldn't afford it on my salary. I might as well admit, too, that I didn't plan to mention this here, because there's only one reason to go to Barreiros at night, and I don't want this to be a dirty novel, although good detective novels do mix crime and sex, mostly in the form of sexual violence. I say that because all the good detective novels I've read are like that. I could name some titles and authors, but they're really well known. You can get them at any magazine stand and even in the supermarket.

But I don't have any choice except to bring up the subject—even though I'm skipping the part about what I did there, which anybody can figure out anyway. I have to explain what happened because it's important to the plot. It has to do with one of the characters, Firmino, the guy who fixes TVs in Santo Anastácio. He works out of two rooms he rents from his father. His place is kind of hard to find, around in back of the church. Firmino's always behind on his bills. Most of the rich people in town send their TVs to the city to get fixed instead of to him. So he's pretty much limited to the business he gets from people who live out on the dirt streets or up on the hill. It's hard for them to pay, and when they do it's in installments, so Firmino ends up working on transistor radios, irons, and vacuum cleaners. His business was on shaky legs from the start. Every time you turn around, he's borrowing money from someone, over at the bar, or the drugstore, or the tax collector's. Once Firmino tried to borrow some money from me, an advance on future repairs. Hey, I don't even have a TV set, why should I lend him money?

But back to the Barreiros business. When I got to Celina's house, the place was packed. It was a Saturday night. The four tables were full, women were running around half-dressed, empty beer bottles were everywhere, the customers were more drunk than happy, and the music was loud enough to make you deaf. Right away I saw it was going to be a wasted trip. The only woman I liked at Celina's already had company: two guys. I was about to leave when I heard somebody yell: "Hey, old buddy, what's up? Come on over here." It was Firmino. At first I didn't like running into him there. I don't like to see people I know in places like that; it makes me uncomfortable. I think it must be some kind of childhood trauma (I read something like that in a magazine once). But there was Firmino, acting like the life of the party. Celina got me a chair and made me sit down. It wasn't how I like to go about things. I'd rather come, do my business, pay and leave, but I thought to myself: if I don't stay, tomorrow nobody's going to be talking about anything else down at the Central. So, even though I didn't really feel like it, I stuck around, drank a few beers, and ended up having a good time, for two reasons: first because I wasn't paying for anything, and second, because the woman I like left her two customers and came over and sat on my lap. Everything turned out fine. After awhile, Firmino, who could barely walk, got up and, hanging on Celina, went to her room. That's when they told me he was the madam's boyfriend.

My Novel Is Not Plagiarism

I read a detective novel once called *The Monastery of Terror*, which actually I didn't like very much, but it had a funny thing: in the beginning there was a list of the characters, one by one, with their professions and other information about them. The title of the list was *dramatis personae*. I could tell it was a fancy term, so I looked it up in the dictionary. It means: set of actors taking part in a play. So I thought of starting my story that way, because it might be nice to mix theater and literature. Of all the novels I've read, it was the only one that started that way. I made up a list and everything, but then I decided not to use it. Since I'd seen that book, probably plenty of critics had too, so when mine came out, they could accuse me of plagiarism. And what's even worse, I would have plagiarized a bad novel. It was one of those really complicated ones with a detective who runs around figuring out clues and making deductions and doesn't get into any fights. (There was one interesting part, though, where the monks beat up some women who were going to be nuns. They had a big orgy with lots of violence, and ended up killing the girls.)

Anyway, I decided not to do the list of characters, but I want to jump ahead a little now and introduce Claudinho, Cirilo's little boy. Cirilo owns a shoe store in the capital. Claudinho was a skinny, eleven-year-old kid with big eyes. I say "was" because he died, and that's what brought out my artistic gift. I knew Claudinho. He was always hanging around the plaza in the afternoon, sometimes with other kids his age. He came to the post office a few times to get stamps for his collection or just to look around. I liked him, he was well-behaved and talked intelligently. Some kids in the city, you have to chase them off when they come around because they're always trying to pull something on you. Not Claudinho. He wanted to know how the mail system worked and why there were so many different stamps worth the same amount. He'd sit there decorating the return addresses on letters and asking about faraway places. I'd always try to have some stamps for him, especially when a new series came out, even if I had to pay out of my own pocket. The kid deserved it. I don't know if I can call him the protagonist of this story, but at any rate, he was the starting point of the whole thing, the reason I'm writing, the source of all the commotion that shook up Santo Anastácio, the cause of all the outrage and sadness that took over the town for several days and, I think, are still felt. If Claudinho isn't the main character, the least I can do is pay my respects here to that poor, innocent kid who was the springboard of my great leap to success.

Visit of the Three Photographers: A Town Topic Because of the Woman

They left the van in the plaza in the morning, and the three occupants wasted no time visiting the nearest houses. They even came to the post office to ask for directions. For my part, I took advantage of their visit to find out who they were and what they were doing in Santo Anastácio. The older one was a professional photographer whose wife, also a photographer, accompanied him, and the young guy was their assistant. I saw their sample albums. Pretty nice. All color pictures. They specialized in child portraits and they brought along props. First, they did one big portrait with the child sitting at a table with a pen in one hand, a book, and a globe, like they have in school, and in the background a map of Brazil. Then they took six 3 by 5s, close-ups from different angles. Then, one more shot, full-length, with a doll for the girls, a plastic machine gun or a ball for the boys. Really nice pictures. If you wanted, you could pay in three installments with no interest charge. The assistant's job was to write up the tickets and have the customers sign. The husband and wife set up the backdrop and took the pictures. They were in town over a week, driving in in the morning and going back at night to a hotel on the highway. They did pretty good business, too.

Nobody paid much attention to them, except for noticing the van had an out-of-state license plate. Then the first story started going around, which was that the car was stolen and the visitors were actually a gang of thieves. The photography was just an excuse to get in people's houses and check everything out. The second story was that when they went inside a house, they waited until nobody was looking and then grabbed whatever was lying around. These rumors, however, were disproved down at the Central. Nobody reported any robberies during the period, and the Chief of Police, Mr. Lourenço, went to the capital to run a check and verified that they really were photographers, licensed and everything, with permits issued in Porto Alegre.

But the third story making the rounds was the most popular—at least in the beginning. The pharmacist claimed that the photographer's wife, who incidentally was very attractive, had another role in the trio's business, one that brought in a lot more income than the photograph albums. He swore he knew all about it: first, the three would go visit a family, and the assistant would take down the name, age, profession, and work address of the man of the house. Then the photographer's wife would get down to business. She'd show up at the place where the guy worked, wearing those tight pants that showed off her hips and behind, and she'd give her sales pitch, trying to persuade the customer to buy an album, and meanwhile dropping hints about how her husband was always working late at night developing negatives, leaving her all alone at the hotel, she being a person who liked to have a good time. Finally the man would figure he couldn't turn this one down and would invite her out to eat. During dinner they'd settle on an extra charge for her "commission." The pharmacist said it was usually double the price of the photo album, but nobody complained because by that time there was hardly anybody left in the restaurant and well . . . you know what I mean, right?

The gang wanted to know how the pharmacist found out about it, and he admitted that she had approached him, but unfortunately he didn't keep their date at the restaurant because he couldn't come up with an excuse to leave the house that night. "So how do you know about the price if you didn't go?" He explained that the next day she came to the drugstore complaining about his not showing up and put the squeeze on him for her taxi fare and waiting at the restaurant. After hearing that, we decided the trio really was using her for bait, but with bait like that, who's going to mind getting hooked. The price wasn't bad, considering the quality of the merchandise. I wouldn't have turned her down, but it was a little steep for me.

The First News and Public Commotion

We were gathered as usual down at the Central. We had two tables pushed together and the whole gang was there, drinking brandy, shots of cane rum, and coffee. It was a cloudy day with a south wind, and the doors of the bar were closed part way. It had been two weeks since the photographers had left town. Since there wasn't anything else to do that evening, we decided to make a tally of all the respectable citizens of Santo Anastácio do Roçado who'd gone out with the shapely photographer. Besides me, the pharmacist was there, the tax collector, Firmino, Peephole (who's Chairman of the City Council), Procópio (who's the opposition party representative), Mr. Lourenço, and the owner of the cafe himself, who wouldn't get out of his chair even when an occasional customer came in, but instead would yell for his wife or daughter to come out and wait table.

Cirilo wasn't there. His name, by the way, appeared on our tally sheet, but he denied having had any contact whatsoever with said female. We had made up our minds that night to make him confess. We knew what day he had gone out with the individual who shall remain unnamed, all we needed was the details, but we wanted to hear them from the horse's mouth. Procópio remarked that Cirilo was late, that he ought to be there already. The tax collector suggested that maybe he had made arrangements with another photographer for the evening, and we were all laughing when in walked Cirilo.

It was eight in the evening by the Central Bar and Cafe's old wall clock, which no longer chimed the hour but still kept good time on its face with faded roman numerals. Cirilo came in and right away started talking to Mr. Lourenço: "Lourenço, my wife's getting worried. I don't want to make too much of it, but I think we'd better do something."

"What happened?"

"It's Claudinho, he didn't come home for dinner, and he still hasn't showed up. I already telephoned the relatives and he's not at any of their houses and I'm getting scared."

"Scared of what, Cirilo?"

"I don't know, I'm just scared. What if he got hit by a car on the highway? I caught him just the other day running across the street without looking, chasing after a bird."

The gang started to talk all at once, everybody making suggestions, and everybody trying to calm Cirilo down; it's nothing, you'll see, the kid probably went over to a friend's house and stayed for dinner, the thing to do is make a list of his friends (that was my idea) and phone or go there in person.

"Well, he doesn't have too many friends here, and my wife already called them."

"And his friends in the capital, classmates?"

"I don't know, there's so many, but Claudinho wouldn't go anywhere without telling his mother and without asking for money. I'm sure he didn't go to the capital. I'm afraid he's been hit by a car."

Mr. Lourenço tried to reassure our friend, and volunteered to go to the police station and call around to the hospitals. Everybody got up to go, even the cafe owner who barely had time to shout at his wife to take over at the counter. We must have totally forgotten about the list of the photographer's admirers, what with something new to think about.

Mercy Hospital said they had an unidentified child in intensive care who had been hit by a car. Cirilo got nervous and said he was in no shape to drive. So everyone got together and we left in two cars, Cirilo's and Mr. Lourenço's.

Some Information about the Chairman of the City Council, Inserted Here Solely for the Purpose of Reducing Tension

Peephole is the oldest City Council member in town. He's finally Chairman now, after serving on the Council for years and years. Profession: municipal inspector, retired. His nickname, Peephole, comes from his first election campaign. They say he had some flyers printed up with his name, a picture of him squeezed into a collar and tie, and the slogan "Candidate of the People." When he got up on the stage set up in the plaza for his first public speech, the joke got started: "The Candidate of the Peep-hole, Peep-hole, Peep-hole!"

Premonition of the Big Moment

On the way back to Santo Anastácio, I was in Cirilo's car with Procópio, Firmino, and the tax collector driving. The whole time, we discussed Claudinho's disappearance, because it turned out the kid in the hospital wasn't him. It was a relief to everyone when Mr. Lourenço and Cirilo returned from intensive care with the news, and we stayed there in the lobby for a while talking and looking at the nurses. I don't know why those nurses don't come down with pneumonia, wearing those skimpy little uniforms, with tennis shoes and bobby socks. Plenty of healthy flesh on exhibit there!

On the way back, Procópio gave a speech about the City Council's responsibility towards the town's children who have a right to play in the plazas and streets with every guarantee of safety and protection. It was about time the Council gave serious thought to putting some guards at the playgrounds and public parks to provide citizens with at least a minimum of security, in line with other towns where city council chairmen truly fulfilled the duties and obligations of the office. I thought Procópio was exaggerating a little, since they don't even have guards like that in the capital, it's the military police that patrol the public parks.

"So why don't they assign us more police?"

I couldn't answer that one, because Procópio was right. All we had, besides the notary public, was one corporal and two soldiers posted at the police station. In the tax collector's opinion, that was more than enough, considering how few crimes there were in Santo Anastácio. Not counting accidents on the highway, which were the Highway Patrol's responsibility, how many robberies did we have? How many fights? How many reports of public disturbances?

I felt we were drifting away from the subject at hand, and I remembered Cirilo's wife: "I wonder how she's doing? Everyone seems to have forgotten about her."

"Look, you guys, here we are talking a lot of nonsense when the kid's probably home with his mother by now."

The others agreed with Firmino, but not me, I sensed something in the air, something different, something whispering in my ear that my big break had come, the story that would become my masterpiece.

The Long Night of Uncertainty and Despair

That night was one of the longest we'd ever spent together. When we got back from the hospital, we went straight in to Cirilo's house, but not everybody came inside. Some stayed in the cars. I went in with Mr. Lourenço and Procópio. When Cirilo's wife saw him without their son, she started sobbing. It was painful to watch, and then she broke into piercing screams. Poor Cirilo, he didn't know what to do, take care of his wife or tell the maid to fix coffee for us. Procópio offered to call the emergency clinic, and I said it'd be a miracle if there was a doctor on call. Everybody knew that weekends and evenings, and holidays too, there were only nurses or maybe a medical student on duty.

Mr. Lourenço called and we lucked out: an intern was there and he came right over. He gave Cirilo's wife a shot, wrote out a prescription, and said that she'd start to calm down in a little while and then would fall asleep. I went out to get the medicine and filled everyone in on what was happening.

Firmino seemed kind of worried and asked if what Cirilo's wife had was serious. The pharmacist told him: "It's nothing, this is just a mild sedative. I don't know why anybody had to call a doctor, I could have told you what to do." I didn't say anything because Tubbs was always prescribing medicine down at the drugstore and lots of people say he cured them.

I went back inside just as Mr. Lourenço was saying he'd take care of everything and that Cirilo should relax and go to bed: tomorrow we'd have news of Claudinho, the boy was probably just over at some friend's house, but, even so, he would take all the necessary measures. We stayed in the living room listening to Cirilo whimpering until Tubbs arrived and we said good-night. There must have been some urge to stay together because nobody said anything about going home. We automatically headed for the Central, which had closed for the night, but where a few lights were still on inside.

The door opened as soon as our noisy group approached, and wife and daughter emerged to ask: "Where were you, Elias? What's going on?"

"Go back to bed, go on, tomorrow I'll tell you all about it, not now, we've got a lot to take care of, go back to bed."

While we settled down inside, he got out the brandy and rum. I remember I didn't get to bed until two in the morning. My head was spinning, I was half asleep, my legs felt weak, and I was seeing things through a kind of fog. I stumbled through the office. In the back room, I kicked one of the canvas mail bags which was full, and fell into bed without undressing. It took me a long time to get to sleep. I kept getting up and lying down. I wandered around the office and drank a lot of water. Finally I got tired, my arms and legs felt like rubber.

Next day I tried to remember what happened the night before. We talked and drank a lot. We were so loud, Elias' wife and daughter had to come out several times and ask us to be quiet, until finally they just stayed up, bringing us drinks and joining in the conversation.

Mr. Lourenço proposed a plan of action which included contacting the nearest police stations and putting announcements on the radio and in the newspapers in the capital. Then he made up a list of questions to ask the residents of Santo Anastácio. Each one of us would be assigned a section of town and this way we would be able to canvas the whole area quickly. Everybody made suggestions, most of them useless, except for one of Peephole's ideas which was that we start by answering the questionnaire ourselves. Procópio's suggestion was unanimously rejected: he wanted to include a question about what people thought about the current City Council Chairman, with regard to public security in the municipality. Anyway, Mr. Lourenço's questions were directed at those who had seen Claudinho that afternoon or evening, and who might know where the boy had been at a certain time, whether he seemed normal or not, who he was with, and so on. Man! I have to give Mr. Lourenço credit, he was impressive, acting just like a detective, the brainy type. Incidentally, I prefer the other kind, the kind that's smart but tough and cool too—and not so old. Nothing against Mr. Lourenço but he's not getting any younger. He has rheumatism, and rumor has it his strength is failing in other ways too, that piece of information coming from his maid, who heard it from his wife, of course, since Mr. Lourenço isn't the type to get involved with maids. I'd like to see him go up against a real criminal. He'd end up in the hospital. Or the cemetery. All the same, the plan he came up with was very creative. Unfortunately, nobody in our group qualified for the questionnaire. It was Elias's daughter who brought some light to that dark night: she remembered that the boy had passed by the cafe around five o'clock that afternoon. She wasn't sure exactly what time it was, but he didn't come back again from wherever he'd been headed. She remembered noticing that he was alone.

Mr. Lourenço Asks an Unexpected Question

The next morning things were still hectic. I left my mail carrier in charge at the post office. Little groups of people were beginning to form in the plaza. Those who knew Mr. Lourenço went to see him at his office at the police station, to ask for or to give information—mostly to ask, because, for the most part, they just wanted to meddle. If Mr. Lourenço weren't such a patient guy, I don't know how many people the soldiers would've run off. The only real information he got was from Claudinho's mother, and it came as a surprise to us that evening at our session at the Central. I repeat: if it weren't for the police chief's composure, for his proverbial patience, things might have taken a different turn, quite possibly for the worse. Again, I have to tip my hat to Mr. Lourenço. Anyone else would have made the biggest fuss Santo Anastácio has ever seen. Not him. He wrote down the information people brought him, was startled, naturally, at some of it, but remained seated at his desk without giving any sign of interest, as calm, cool, and collected as could be.

The morning passed and he saw more people in the afternoon. He directed "Operation Questionnaire" with great attention to detail, not to mention our collaboration (I couldn't help much because the post office was busy, it seemed everybody decided to mail a letter that day). He phoned other police stations, giving orders in his usual firm, low voice.

The sad truth is that everything confirmed Claudinho's disappearance. No good news. Cirilo took his wife to stay with family in the capital, returning right away and shutting himself up with Mr. Lourenço at the police station for a good half hour.

We all got together much earlier than usual that evening at Elias' cafe, even though we didn't start in seriously on the Claudinho affair until after the regulars and other stray customers had left. Elias was too busy to join us for about three hours;

people kept coming in, unfamiliar faces, asking questions and making comments, but they didn't get a word out of us! We just made small talk without giving anything away, and tried to pick up any piece of information we hadn't heard already. When things quieted down, Elias got rid of the stragglers and closed the restaurant. We were all set now to go at it uninterrupted.

Right off, we started talking about the day's take, which was a lot more than usual, and we'd just begun when Mr. Lourenço called for silence and took the podium: "Well then, my friends, this is no simple matter to deal with. The possibilities are numerous and I don't want to be hasty. Right now, all we know is that the boy has disappeared. We can't afford to dismiss any detail, any piece of information, no matter how far-fetched it might seem. We have to follow up every lead, even the most ridiculous ones. It's the only way to find out what happened. Let's hope for the best, and not get carried away with wild ideas now. What we're dealing with is a case of a child who left home and hasn't returned yet. It happens all the time, all over Brazil, every day. The problem is that it happened here, to the son of one of our friends. What we need to do is reconstruct the boy's movements, as closely as possible, from the time he left the house. There's no other way to begin."

Mr. Lourenço's speech had an excellent effect on the group. We all listened attentively. It was like a meeting of mutes. I thought he had made a fine start, and I wondered if he ever read detective novels. There he was, the calm detective, a puzzle set out before him, ready to start the game, the shuffled pieces spread out on the table.

And what does Mr. Lourenço do but take the first piece and put it in place: "What I'm going to say now stays in this room. You noticed Cirilo isn't here tonight. I insisted he stay home so he wouldn't hear this, get upset and ruin everything." I glanced quickly around the room. Tubbs the pharmacist, his little coffee cup sitting there in front of him, was looking at Mr. Lourenço. For that matter, everyone was looking at the chief. Everyone but Elias, who was draining his glass of brandy. Firmino's lips seemed to be trembling slightly, the tax collector was adjusting his glasses, Peephole was crossing and uncrossing his legs, Procópio was scratching his nose. I thought: maybe the police chief is onto something. I stared hard at him.

He repeated: "I want you to promise you won't say anything about this to anyone. We'll discuss it only here among ourselves." And to Elias: "Go check on your wife and daughter, make sure they don't come out and hear, all right?" Elias got up and shut the door to the rest of the house.

"After all the talk I heard today, I got only one solid piece of information. The source is Claudinho's mother, but even so I have to confirm it. What she said this morning came as a surprise to me because it was something that should already have been said, and guess where? Right here, last night. That's why I kept it to myself and want you to keep it to yourselves too. This is for our ears only, understand?"

Nobody spoke, but it was understood we all agreed.

"Virginia told me that when Claudinho left home that afternoon, he had a specific destination in mind, nowhere important, just a place like any other place, somewhere anybody might go. But what really bothers me is that last night, one of you could have told us where that boy went."

All of a sudden, the atmosphere got thick. Everyone looked at everyone else. Nobody spoke, we just waited for the bomb to fall. Procópio took a gulp of his rum. Elias got up again and went to get Mr. Lourenço more coffee. The tax collector took off his glasses and wiped them with his handkerchief. Mr. Lourenço took his time drinking the coffee. Only when he finished the cup, did he resume: "What time was Claudinho in your shop yesterday afternoon, Firmino?"

An Addendum in Favor of the *Ventral Decubitus*

I already said that my premonition of the big moment, of that inspiration I'd been waiting for so long, came to me the night we returned from the hospital. That's partly true, although I must confess that before closing the office that afternoon, I was sitting at my desk, counting up the receipts, when—just like that—I had a vision. I almost wrote it down. It was the outline of a novel in which the criminal doesn't get caught. It's probably fair to say that it was at that precise moment that I first felt the inspiration for the book I'm now writing. To be more exact, though, I should say it was at that instant the muse struck. The receipt book was there in my hands, but I wasn't even aware of it. My mind was reeling with words that were like bits of printed pages. It was the book I'd longed for. The victim fallen on the *ventral decubitus,* and the killer in the shadows, his face hidden. A parenthesis: the expression *ventral decubitus* is something I found in a news article a long time ago. It was the first and only time I've seen the term used in the crime pages to describe the position of a prone body. Victims of crime tend to fall on the *dorsal decubitus,* why I don't know. My victim would fall on the *ventral decubitus,* and thus I would be the second author to employ the term. I didn't notice how long I was under the spell of these literary thoughts. When I came to, it was already after six o'clock. I tidied up and closed the office.

The Response That Caused a Variety of Reactions

Firmino turned pale. The question had caught him off-guard. Before he could answer, Tubbs let out with an unprintable exclamation, and Peephole said: "Fir-mi-no!" Just about everybody tried to talk at the same time, as if we wanted to respond, to answer for him, or what's probably closer to the truth, to reproach him and demand an explanation. Mr. Lourenço asserted his authority and order was restored: "You've got the floor, Firmino, and the rest of you, listen up, nobody interrupt."

Firmino began: "Look, I didn't think it was important, it was a minor thing . . ."

"The time, Firmino, what time was it!"

"Oh, well, the boy was there . . . I mean . . . it must have been about five o'clock, I think, maybe a little after. He was only there for a second and then he left . . ."

"Are you sure about the time, Firmino?"

"No, Mr. Lourenço, I'm not positive, but it was a little after I was in here for a bite to eat, so it must have been about five o'clock, a little past five."

"All right, let's say it was five o'clock or five after, that's question number one; now, why did he go there?"

"He stopped by to see if their portable television set was ready. I picked it up a few days ago, it didn't have any picture, just sound . . ."

"How long was he in your shop?"

"He didn't stay long, he came in, asked about the TV, and left. The TV wasn't ready, I hadn't bought the picture tube for it. I've been kind of broke lately ('As usual,' the tax collector murmured). I even asked Cirilo for a loan, but he turned me down."

Mr. Lourenço didn't ask any more questions. He leaned back in his chair, looking at Firmino.

Elias brought the chief some more coffee, Peephole grumbled "I don't believe this," and Procópio began lodging a formal complaint against Firmino for lying, dishonesty, withholding information from the authorities, and indirect complicity in a criminal act. The tax collector turned to me and said he thought the situation demanded further investigation. If Firmino, the defendant, could have found a hole under the table, he would have crawled into it.

In the midst of the confusion, Mr. Lourenço raised his calm, deliberate voice: "Let's not get excited, everybody, calm down now, you're making this out to be worse than it is. Let's just take it easy. I'm satisfied with Firmino's statement. It confirms exactly what I already knew, only it had to be verified, that's all. You all look like you've seen a ghost. Remember, Firmino's one of us. It's perfectly understandable that he would have forgotten the incident, or, and I can understand this too, that he'd be reluctant to mention it later. Wouldn't you? Think about it, was there any specific reason why the incident should have been brought up?"

After that, the group cooled off. Everybody was asking Mr. Lourenço questions and, after a little bit, he gave his assessment of the situation: "The information we have at this point doesn't help much, except we know the boy was alive and here in Santo Anastácio right under our noses, yesterday at five o'clock."

I asked: "So do you think he's dead?"

"I haven't formulated anything you could call a theory yet, first we have to conduct an investigation, and that's what we're doing, agreed?"

We agreed.

And he went on: "In order to solve a problem, one has to start by putting things in order, that is, by systematically organizing all the elements at one's disposal, and by being as realistic as possible, not asking for miracles but using good sense. This is absolutely fundamental." Mr. Lourenço paused and stood there beaming at us. I understood how pleased he was with his philosophical speech. Then, abruptly, he continued: "Instead of clearing things

up, what we have now is a question: When Claudinho passed by
the bar here, as Elias's daughter says she saw, was he coming back
from Firmino's shop, or was he on his way there?"

Excitement Stirred Up by Memories and a Nocturnal Visit

Our meeting broke up as late as the night before. I got back to
my room after two A.M. again, but this time steady on my feet
because I had only had coffee. My head, on the other hand, was
spinning. The last thing Mr. Lourenço said had stirred me up, for
two reasons, the first being that I couldn't figure out what he was
getting at. What did it matter whether Claudinho was coming or
going when Elias' daughter saw him? Why would that be important? I couldn't see that it made any difference. I sat down on the
edge of the bed and tried to analyze it, but I couldn't come up
with a plausible explanation. If he was coming back from the shop
it was because he'd already been there, and if he was going, he'd
end up getting there. So what? . . . It just seemed like some silly
game to me, where the little black and white pieces move forward
or backwards however many squares the dice and the rules allow.
   The other thing that had me hot and bothered was the thought
of Elias' daughter, in pants and a tight wool sweater now because
of the cold, but in summer, man, those teeny tiny shorts, hitched
up high so you can see her buns. She wasn't even there at the bar,
so why did Mr. Lourenço have to bring her up.? I was doing fine
until I started thinking about her. I was worried that Elias had
started keeping an eye on me when she was around. I took off my
clothes, quickly put on my pijamas, turned out the light, and got
under the covers.
   I lay there on my back without moving, waiting for the bed to
warm up. I was looking at the ceiling, my hands between my legs
which were drawn up together. A pleasant warmth began spread-
ing little by little up to my neck. Light from the street filtered in
through the window blinds in the office, passed through the open
doorway and made delicate patterns on the dark wall in front of
me. Shadows waved on the rectangle of wall, ghosts (friends or
enemies?) prowled around the building. Strange animals, snakes
or bats—bat-snakes—crawled from my head and tried to get in my
stomach, take root there inside, gnaw on my intestines, rip out my

hot, erect virility. Dancers softly slithered about the room, like the snakes coiled around my chest, squeezing, speeding my pulse, increasing the pressure. Me, immobile, eyes open, waiting.

Silently, she approached, began taking off her blouse, her bra, holding her breasts out like an offering of firm ripe fruit, removing the last piece of clothing, brushing it away with her foot, bending over my burning face, the better to breathe in that perfume of fresh roses. The fever took over, I surrendered to her warm body, I let it ride a wild, violent gallop that tore from me a quick shudder of pleasure. When I woke up the next day and opened the office, the mail carrier was already waiting on the doorstep. He asked if I was sick.

Following Firmino

It was the third day, and still little progress had been made on the case, although we had found out one or two things. I spent my time hanging around the plaza, going to the office only when the mail carrier couldn't handle something himself.

In the morning, with nothing special in mind, I decided to take a turn around the church. I noticed Firmino's shop was closed. It was after nine o'clock. I wondered where he was. I went over to the drugstore. Tubbs came out from behind the counter and sat down with me, taking up two of the three chairs set out for customers.

"What do you think about what Mr. Lourenço said last night, about Firmino's holding out about the kid being there?" he asked me.

It was a great opportunity for me to repeat the chief's remark, which I thought was very well put: "I haven't formulated a theory yet, in order to have a theory you have to investigate first, and that's what we're doing, right?" Of course. But I added: "Even without trying, sometimes you find things out. Just now, in fact, I was over behind the church and Firmino's shop is closed. Have you seen him?"

Tubbs looked at me with suspicion written all over his face and said no. "Stay here a minute, okay? I'm going to run over to the tax collector's, I'll be right back." And he took off.

I sat there chuckling to myself, knowing that Tubbs would pass on what I'd told him, and that in a little while the group would know that Firmino wasn't at work that morning. As soon as Tubbs got back, I left. As I was crossing the plaza, I saw Firmino leave the police station and head for the bus stop. I sat down on a bench and watched until the bus came and he got on.

The Whys and Wherefores of Comings and Goings

It wasn't until that afternoon that I stopped by the police station for a minute. Mr. Lourenço invited me into his office. "Nothing new on the western front," he told me, "it's turned into a routine investigation of a disappearance. I called Cirilo. His wife is better, although she's very depressed. He's still going to work, but he's pretty upset, poor guy, he doesn't know who to turn to. I told him that in a case like this there's nothing to do but wait. We're doing everything we can."

"I know you're doing everything you can, but tell me, what do you think really happened to the boy? Where did he go?"

"Frankly, Jerônimo, I don't want to be too pessimistic, but we don't know if he went somewhere or if he was taken, you understand? Do you know how many children are kidnapped every day, the world over?"

No, I didn't know, and he didn't tell me.

"Do you know how many children are never found?"

No, I didn't know. And he didn't tell me that, either.

"All we can do, Jerônimo, is be patient. I'm sorry for the parents in a case like this, but we have to be patient. Sometimes when you least expect it the loose end falls into place and the puzzle is solved."

"Mr. Lourenço, I wanted to ask you a question."

"What's that?"

"Yesterday, you talked about the shop and Claudinho coming or going, what does all that mean?"

"It means a great deal, my boy, a great deal. You mean you haven't figured that out yet? All right, pay attention. It's important because it's a clue to where Claudinho was that day. But I'm convinced now that when he passed by the cafe, he was coming back from the workshop. Having analyzed the problem carefully, I'm sure I'm right."

"You're positive?"

"Positive. He had to be returning. According to what Virginia told me, after lunch that afternoon Claudinho went out to the garage to play marbles with the neighbor's boy, saying he'd do his chores later on in the evening. They played together until about four o'clock, or a little later, when they stopped to have a snack. Up to that point, nothing out of the ordinary. After the snack, Claudinho wanted to watch one of his favorite movies on TV, but he wanted to watch it in the garage so they could go on playing. Since the portable TV was at Firmino's getting fixed, he left, saying he was going to the shop to get the TV. Now, we know that the street his house is on comes out above the plaza. From there, the direct route to the shop would be straight along the side of the street the church is on, you follow me? So, to pass by Elias's bar, on the way to the shop, he would have had to take an unnecessary detour, going all the way around the plaza or crossing it at some point, and I don't think he would have done that. Don't forget he wanted to see his movie, so he was in a hurry. See what I mean?"

I saw, all right. What he was telling me was that Claudinho left the shop and went somewhere else.

"And then, Mr. Lourenço?"

"That's what we have to find out, where he went afterwards, otherwise we're back at square one. His destination is what seems to me to be the key to the problem."

"But, Mr. Lourenço," I hazarded, "what if the boy decided to go by the movie house to see what was playing, wouldn't he have taken the longer route?"

Mr. Lourenço just looked at me and didn't say anything, so I left. I didn't have the nerve to ask him what Firmino was doing earlier at the police station.

Behind the Veil

The room was filled with the fading light of dusk. The lamp was not on and the strange light that filtered through the dirty glass of the little window was not enough to see clearly inside. The door to the other room was closed. The boy, standing next to a crude table, seemed to be unaware of the man behind him, whose shadowed face was tense, the eyes half-closed. Without making a sound, the man reached down and picked up the iron bar at his feet. The child seemed to be totally absorbed, occupied with something on the table. The man took two steps forward and, without looking, swung the iron bar down. Struck on the back of the neck, the child, without even a gasp, grabbed on to the table before he fell, pulling it a few centimeters toward him. The man examined the inert body. A little blood was coming from the wound, making a small puddle on the floor. A thin red thread also ran from his ear. He was still breathing weakly. The killer struck once more on the head. He stepped back, put the weapon down next to the wall, and left immediately, locking the door behind him.

The Second Disappearance

Our meeting that night took on considerable significance, despite the fact that Cirilo and Firmino were absent. Or maybe because of it. It was easy to see the eagerness on our faces, each one trying to conceal it by putting on an unconcerned air that didn't fool anyone. Mr. Lourenço had become the center of attention, our leader, although he hadn't been officially elected yet. Cirilo's absence wasn't any surprise, we knew he was staying in the capital for a few days, but Firmino's not being there aroused our curiosity.

The tax collector was the first one to speak up: "Hey, where's Firmino?"

And Tubbs: "He wasn't at work this morning."

Elias: "This afternoon he stopped in for a drink but I don't know whether he went to work after that."

"He didn't," the pharmacist cut in, "I checked and he wasn't there."

Procópio: "Look, it's the chief who can tell us what's going on."

And Peephole: "Now I suppose you're going to tell us everybody's disappearing around here?"

A New Theory Develops

During this exchange, everybody's eyes were glued to Mr. Lourenço, who didn't wait to have his arm twisted: "It's obvious all of you know by now that Firmino was at the police station this morning, as if we didn't have the most efficient information dissemination system in the state (laughter). But what you don't know and what you want to know is why he was there, am I right or not?"

And turning to Elias: "Elias, lock the door . . ."

"Don't worry, they went to the movies tonight."

"Good. Now then, needless to say, I hold you to the promise that what we talk about here doesn't leave this room, okay? Firmino came to my office to tell me in confidence about something he saw that night which might be important, but since it was so vague and there was no guarantee it had any bearing on the case, he was afraid to speak up. I'm sure you all understand. He told me that the day Claudinho disappeared, he, Firmino, was having lunch at the barbecue place out on the highway. He saw a van parked there, and he thought it looked like the one the photographers had, you remember them, right? Now, this didn't seem very important at the time, and he didn't see the photographers in the restaurant. However, on the way out, he ran into the photographers' assistant, who quickly turned away, as if he didn't want to be seen. At the time, Firmino didn't make the connection, but later he remembered those stories about them being thieves, and, finally, he decided to report it to me. And that's what he did."

A small debate ensued. Over why Firmino had only decided to report the incident after three days had gone by. About whether there was a link between the assistant being in Santo Anastácio and Claudinho's disappearance, after the photographers had been gone for over two weeks? Old Firmino seemed to know an awful lot about everything! And he sure was keeping a lot to himself!

It was then that I almost added fuel to the fire unintentionally by remembering how I had run into Firmino at Celina's house, something I hadn't told anyone about. Since nobody knew about Firmino's loose living, nor about his status in the red light district, if I had mentioned it then and there, it would have been a big mess. It was a good thing I kept my mouth shut. Firmino was in enough hot water already.

Mr. Lourenço decided to pour a little cold water on the fire: "Now, I don't see anything strange about the photographers' van returning to Santo Anastácio, because, after all, how do we know people didn't still owe them money? It would be perfectly natural for the assistant to come back to collect the money, while the photographers did business in another city."

"So then why is Firmino trying to put ideas in people's heads?" Peephole asked.

"He's not putting anything in anybody's head, all he did was pass on to me a piece of information that he felt he ought to, especially since I made it clear to him that I didn't like his keeping quiet about Claudinho's visit to his shop. What would you have done in his place? Wouldn't you come running to me with any scrap of information you came across?"

Mr. Lourenço was right. He was always right. But I couldn't resist: "So why isn't Firmino here tonight?"

"Does he have to come every night? Look here, sometimes one of you . . ."

I returned to the attack: "Mr. Lourenço, do you suppose the photographers have something to do with the case?"

"Anybody could, provided we consider the disappearance a kidnapping, for example."

A kidnapping? I could see the guys were impressed. "Do you think it might be a kidnapping?"

"Probably not. I think it's more likely the boy ran away and joined some other runaways in the capital, and is afraid to return. That's normal under the circumstances, children are afraid of possible punishment on their return, so they stay where they are, or keep running. What one has to do is what was done in this case: communicate with the police in the area, with the press, and with the juvenile authorities. Sometimes a runaway will show up just like that, but it's the duty of a police officer not to dismiss alternative theories. It's possible our Claudinho has been kidnapped. Cirilo isn't penniless, so it's a possibility, although in that case, it's odd that no message has arrived from the kidnappers."

The Letter That Didn't Come in the Mail

The next morning, Cirilo's maid found an envelope on the floor when she was straightening up the living room. It had been slipped under the door sometime during the night. It was addressed: "To Mr. Cirilo." She called her boss who came immediately. Letter in hand, he took off for the police station. Following

on his heels were the neighbors, and behind them, whoever happened to be in the plaza at the time, and behind them, Tubbs,
Elias, Firmino, the tax collector, the vicar, and the janitor at the
movie theater. Me. Two minutes later, Peephole, Procópio, the
entire majority party coalition, the Mayor and his Secretary of
Health, Education, and Public Works, the representative of the
opposition party, and my mail carrier, whom I sent running back
to the post office because it can't be left unattended even in cases
of national emergency.

Mr. Lourenço had his hands full getting everybody out of the
police station. He assigned two soldiers to guard the entrance and
stationed the corporal at his office door. Following Mr. Lourenço
inside were Cirilo, the notary, the Mayor, and naturally, his Secretary of Health, Education, and Public Works, the Chairman of the
City Council, the vicar, and the representative of the opposition
party. Everybody else, out on the street. Over the protests of the
majority party representative, who saw Procópio's being allowed
in as an odious form of discrimination, an improper privilege
awarded by the authority of the police, guardian of the people's
most sacred interests, the one institution that cannot show favor-
itism. That insensitive gesture meant giving in to subversive elements which would now infiltrate the seat of government itself.

I was there, next to the corporal, waiting to see what the upshot
of it all would be. Cirilo's neighbors had already taken it upon
themselves to spread the news, and it was passed rapidly from
mouth to mouth. A kidnapping! The outlaws were demanding a
ransom of a hundred thousand. A hundred thousand or a hundred million? Could Cirilo come up with a hundred million? A
hundred thousand isn't much. What do you mean it isn't much,
how many people in Santo Anastácio ever see that much money in
their whole lives?

A hundred thousand, Cirilo would later confirm. The letter,
which was typed, said the following: "Have ready a hundred
thousand cruzeiros if you want your son back, we will send more
instructions later."

For half an hour, the crowd stayed in the plaza, hoping something else would happen. When Mr. Lourenço appeared at the
door, everybody pressed forward and the buzzing grew to a roar.
With a wave of his hand, he invoked a respectful silence. Or one
thirsty for news. The statement he made was simple, straightfor-

ward, and produced an immediate effect: "I'll give you people five minutes to get back to what you were doing. I just called the capital and in a little bit a squad of military police will be here. So I want the streets cleared, everybody go on home. You already know what happened, there's nothing else to find out. The rest is for the police to attend to, so make yourselves scarce while there's still time. If the police pick you up I won't take responsibility for what happens, and all of you know what'll happen, so clear out."

A few people took off running, others left slowly, acting brave (I'd like to see them when the police show up with their rubber clubs, then we'd see how brave they are). One small group went over to the drugstore. The janitor from the movie theater ran across and locked both doors before it occurred to anyone to hide in there. He locked himself in. The Mayor, accompanied by his Secretary of Health, Education, and Public Works, crossed the plaza in the direction of the courthouse, and the last group of rubberneckers followed behind, listening to the Mayor explain the terms of the letter and the measures that were being taken, and make the promise that "the city government would not be ex . . . clud . . . ex . . . cu . . . ded" (the mayor had a little trouble with his word, but the Secretary of Health, Education and Public Works came to his rescue) "ex-clu-ded from the investigation process." I went off with Firmino. To this day, the squad of military police has yet to appear.

Postscriptum

The opposition party coalition was not summoned specifically on the occasion of the arrival of the letter because it is summed up in the person of its leader, Procópio. The other member is Emiliano, alias One-Step due to the fact that he limps around on one leg, who is on leave of absence for an indefinite period of time because of health reasons. He's at the Santana Clinic, recovering from perennial and excessive alcohol consumption, and the only alternate refused to take over because he was elected Head Municipal Street Sweeper, and it is inappropriate for an elected official, entrusted with an important office, to come out in open and direct opposition to the Mayor. That's why I only mentioned the representative of the opposition party.

A Heretofore Little-Known Side of Firmino

While he worked with the tool, soldering together little metal parts and wires, Firmino explained to me why he wasn't at work or at our meeting yesterday. He repeated the story I already knew about the photographers' assistant, and he added a few things in confidence, after I swore I wouldn't pass them on to anyone. The reason he, Firmino, had gone to the Police Chief was that he felt, the very moment he saw the guy there at the barbecue place trying to hide, that something funny was going on. And if the photographers were criminal types anyway? It was just one step from stealing to kidnapping children. This was the thought that had come to him. He couldn't explain why, it was an intuitive thing, something that just happens. "You know what I mean."

"What do you mean?"

"I mean when a message comes to you out of nowhere, like a spirit, a sort of a guide that's trying to help and talks to you, you know?"

"Yes, I knew, but I didn't say anything. I always stayed away from supernatural voodoo stuff like that. I was invited one time to a voodoo church, but I was afraid to go. That's the truth: I was afraid. That invisible stuff scares me. What if it's really true? I say let the dead stay dead and leave me in peace and goodwill on earth (From ghoulies and ghosties, deliver us!)

"Well, that's what it was like, it came floating through my ears and into my head like a breeze. I'm sure it was that half-Indian guy down in my neighborhood who talks to spirits. I didn't mention that to the chief, because he doesn't believe in that stuff and he doesn't approve. He might try to get me in trouble. I only told him about getting suspicious when I saw the assistant photographer."

"But Firmino, don't you think bringing it up like that is kind of dangerous? Just because the guy was there that day doesn't mean he kidnapped Claudinho."

Firmino was convinced the photographers had some kind of criminal record, and if they weren't involved in the boy's disappearance, they were at least mixed up in some robbery or drug deal. "Nobody turns away and tries to hide like he did if he isn't guilty of something. I'll tell you something else, Jerônimo, I trust my intuition, and if those guys cross my path, I give you my word

I'll kill them, because one thing I won't stand for is seeing a child hurt."

Having said that, he grabbed my arm and stealthily opened one of the drawers in his worktable: "You see that?" In the middle of a mountain of wire was a gun. "See that? I know you won't tell anybody. I trust you. It's right here waiting and you better believe I'm ready to use it, if it comes to that I'll go out and hunt those filthy animals down myself. I'll wipe them off the face of the earth before I'll stand by and let them touch one hair on that little boy's head."

"Look, Firmino, what you do is your business. Don't worry, I didn't see a thing: deaf, dumb and blind, okay? But my advice is, don't do it. Helping Mr. Lourenço is one thing, but going out and shooting these guys . . . come on, you don't want to do that. What about your family? You have a family, don't you?"

"I had one, yeah, but you know, I've been separated from my wife for a long time. I don't even like to think about her" (I know, you bum, all you want to think about now is Celina!).

"Don't worry, just leave it to me. I wasn't fooling around yesterday when I spent the day with a friend of mine, somebody I trust completely, getting the gun" (Ah! so you spent all day with the madam, huh, Firmino!).

"This gun is that child's revenge. See, if they hurt him, then everything makes sense."

"What makes sense?"

"The kidnapping and the letter. They're after money, so they took the kid and now they're threatening the father. He's got to pay the money or pay the price, that's how it is. What I'm afraid is they won't turn over the kid after they get the money. But I'm not going to worry about that yet, that's when my gun comes into the picture."

The little man seemed to have his mind made up. Was it right for me to keep his secret? Or should I tell Mr. Lourenço? I thought about it for a minute, and decided to keep my mouth shut. It wasn't my problem. Firmino was already dead set on the idea. If he wanted to put a bullet in somebody, as long as it wasn't me, let him do it, who cares. If the photographers really were criminals, then they deserved to be punished and it didn't matter who did it. As I was leaving, I noticed in the corner of the shop an enormous black cat stretched out in a wooden box full of sand.

She was nursing a large litter of kittens. Not that too! As if voodoo and having homicidal tendencies weren't enough, Firmino turns out to keep cats too.

Behind the Veil Continued

About fifteen minutes later the man returned to the room where his victim lay on the floor. He pulled the shades down and turned on the ceiling light. He examined the room carefully and was satisfied. Everything was there. He rolled the body up in a dirty bath towel and bound it with wire. He dragged the bundle into a corner and went into the bathroom, from which he emerged with some old rags and a plastic bucket of water. A second inspection. The next task was to stuff the body inside a heavy cloth bag, put the piece of iron inside, and tie it closed.

Accusations by the People's Representative

Mr. Lourenço wasn't at the police station that afternoon. He left the corporal and the notary there to tell anyone who asked that he'd gone to the capital, specifically to the Bureau of Public Safety. We, the poor mortals of Santo Anastácio do Roçado, were left exercising our right to cultivate the grapevine, receiving and passing along the latest rumors, and keeping one eye glued to the police station because Mr. Lourenço might return any time and who wanted to miss that?

Around four o'clock, a VW bug pulled up in front of the police station and two guys jumped out, one of them with his jacket tossed over his shoulder, holding a camera in one hand. They turned out to be journalists from *The Statesman,* the oldest newspaper in the capital and the one with the largest circulation. They went inside but immediately came back out. The photographer took a few shots of the plaza, the Courthouse, little groups of people, and then a few more of those who had gathered around him. They headed toward Cirilo's house which was closed up, not even the maid was there. They took more pictures and talked to the people hanging around.

Among those interviewed was the worthy representative of the people, Procópio, the opposition party council chairman, whose statements were the subject of considerable discussion the next day when they appeared in the newspapers. He virtually accused the city authorities, including our police chief, of neglecting their official duties. He didn't mention Mr. Lourenço by name, but he implied that the chief was to blame for failing to exercise the proper caution with regard to the appearance of strangers in town. If he had been more vigilant, the child photographers would not have escaped the long arm of the law and a lot of things would be cleared up, because from the time they first appeared in Santo Anastácio, the authorities had been aware of certain doubts as to the photographers' intentions, of growing suspicions concerning their activities, of the possibility they had been involved in specific robberies committed in the capital. All the troubles which had afflicted our prosperous if poorly served city, could have been avoided by simply detaining the outsiders or placing them under strict surveillance. Well known and respectable citizens had good reason to believe it was indeed the fraudulent photographers who were responsible for kidnapping the innocent boy, the favorite child of a distinguished and honorable businessman from the capital, whose decision to make Santo Anastácio do Roçado his home was a source of pride and satisfaction to the town. Those were Procópio's words.

A Mournful Mood

Cirilo was present at our regular gathering at the end of that day of turmoil, with the press showing up, people running around all over the place, the police chief gone, and all the talk about the kidnapping and what to do. Everybody had an opinion. There were dozens of ideas and dozens of solutions. What Procópio told the reporters circulated around town, enriched by suggestive or pious elaborations. Down at the Central, after we sorted everything out and analyzed it, the main conclusions we arrived at were that the three photographers were involved, that the police needed to act energetically and quickly, that the child could already be dead or suffering incalculable physical and moral damage, that the criminals had to be caught at all costs, and that doing things like that to an innocent child would not be tolerated.

Mr. Lourenço did not endorse our conclusions, but chose instead to listen and interrupt with questions like, are you sure?

Cirilo was obviously upset. He couldn't keep his hands still. When he wasn't rubbing them together, he was scratching his chin, his cheek, his nose. He drank I don't know how many coffees and smoked as many cigarettes. He was determined to get the Chief's word on whether he should pay the amount they had demanded, and whether the police would or wouldn't try to follow the kidnappers.

In the bar, the tables were full of people watching us. In a low voice, so the other customers wouldn't hear (and who didn't try to get in on the case? If they could have, they would have followed the Chief to the bathroom), Mr. Lourenço said he couldn't talk there, that if we wanted to talk, we'd have to leave discreetly and go somewhere else. I proposed we regroup at the post office. Mr. Lourenço agreed and planned a strategy. I was the first to leave, then the others, one by one, at regular intervals. The last was Elias, who brought along a bottle of brandy.

The guys settled down as best they could because there weren't enough chairs to go around. I put water on for coffee and sat down on the floor. As an extra precaution to guarantee we were safe and wouldn't be interrupted during the task ahead, Mr. Lourenço told the soldier on duty to keep an eye on the post office.

Still, Mr. Lourenço was calmer than the rest of us. He tried to comfort Cirilo by saying there was an awful lot of talk going around, but it was just speculation. There was no reason to get ruffled about nothing. If the boy was in the hands of the photographers, he would be rescued. Why did Cirilo think Mr. Lourenço had gone to the capital that afternoon? To go sightseeing? He had gone to inform higher authorities of the latest developments. The Bureau of Public Safety was already on the job, Cirilo could rest easy on that score. Why, at that very moment, as we were talking, special agents were being deployed. The letter had been sent to the technical experts. Why torment yourself? Let people talk, but please, let's not encourage more talk, we could count on him and on the police. Those responsible would be caught sooner or later and the boy was sure to be found.

Cirilo was crushed, and I felt sorry for him. We could all see he was on the point of breaking down completely. His head bowed, listening to Mr. Lourenço's sermon, Cirilo looked totally devastated. What was he thinking about at that moment? How does a father feel when suddenly, without explanation, he finds himself without his only child, his own flesh and blood, his promise of immortality? I'm not a father so I can't describe with any reasonable accuracy the shock that Cirilo must have been experiencing. I don't even know if it was shock. All I can say is that I felt for him. I realize it's a cliché to say somebody aged ten years in a few days, but Cirilo had aged. Only four days had gone by, and there were deep lines in the man's face that hadn't been there before. His hair had lost its natural shine, his eyes were dull, and the corners of his mouth turned down. It was a typical portrait of a human being consumed by suffering. A martyr. I felt sorry for the poor guy. I went over to him and impulsively gave him a pat on the head. He seemed to understand. He lifted his eyes to me, speechless, a rictus that tried to be a smile on his face. He took my hand in his and I had the sensation he was going to lick it—like a little wounded animal! I left and went to serve the coffee.

Disarming the Accuser

"The fact that the photographers had left Santo Anastácio doesn't pose a problem, especially since, as Firmino said, the assistant was here that sad afternoon," Mr. Lourenço resumed. "Don't forget, it's only been four days since it all started. And remember, after they left, they continued their normal routine for two weeks, in order to avoid attracting attention. Then they executed their plan, which must have been simple: while the husband and wife conduct business as usual in some town nearby, the assistant returns, leaves the van on the outskirts of town, at the barbecue place, where nobody will pay much attention to it. He watches and waits, and then follows the boy and, somehow or other, grabs him. Nobody in town would notice him, especially in the early evening when the streets are practically deserted. Based on the business they did here in Santo Anastácio, and considering they would travel only on paved roads, it's not hard to figure out where they went. They had to go either north or south, and in this case, however fast they worked, they couldn't have gotten farther than Tubarão or Itajaí. Let's add a safety margin and include

Crisciúma and Blumenau. Now then, my friends, that's not too big an area for the police to cover, is it? Why so much concern, then, as if the kidnappers were lost in the Amazon? And even if they were, do you think for one minute we don't have the means to catch them there? Even if they went to China, my dear friends, all the way to China!"

Procópio, I might add, was at a loss for words. More than once he tried to interrupt, but Mr. Lourenço wouldn't give him a chance. Firmino visibly approved of the Police Chief's theory and bobbed his head up and down: yes! yes! The others looked at Cirilo, then at Procópio.

Peephole put in his two bits: "Well, that's what happens when certain politicians run for office, if the law were tougher this wouldn't happen, this subversion everywhere, this . . ." The phrase was left hanging in the air. Peephole had made one of the longest and most substantial speeches of his career. Never had he spoken at such length at the City Council.

Procópio looked at him but, although it was hard to believe, said nothing. Any other time he would have sunk his teeth in. But Mr. Lourenço's statement had disarmed Procópio. It was like saying: You're making a big fuss over nothing, it's just cheap demagoguery. And that's how it turned out, too. Mr. Lourenço called the newspapers and before you knew it, it was done, all the Chief had to do was pick up the phone!

Under the Sign of Urea

I walked the guys outside. It was after midnight. There wasn't a soul in the plaza. Just like Tubbs always says: after the movie lets out, Santo Anastácio is a ghost town, you could walk around naked and nobody would care. The guys went their separate ways. Mr. Lourenço stopped by the police station, probably to wake up the soldier on duty. Over at town hall only the front porch light was on. The watchman was no doubt performing his duties by sleeping on the sofa in the Mayor's outer office—a watchdog guarding the door to his master's chambers. The damp air made the deep green grass and leaves sparkle like thousands of little stars twinkling in the weak glow from the three streetlights on the plaza.

The light bulb in the bedroom had burned out more than a month ago. I stood in front of the post office for a long time, absorbing the silence, the peace, the enormous emptiness. The waves in the bay were calm and black. I felt like walking over to the dirty beach behind the houses, or to the jetty to see the capital in the distance, clearly reflected on the other side. I felt like taking off my clothes and crossing the plaza, roaming the streets, naked, completely naked, to see if anyone would notice, if some old insomniac spinster was looking out her window, waiting for the naked man in her life, or—who knows——waiting for an angel (or a devil) to appear and add a little spice to her vigil. That's how I felt.

I crossed the street and stood in the middle of the plaza, in front of one of the lawns where, a few days before, the soil had been turned and fertilized. That's how I felt. I urinated long and hard on the soft ground, watering the seedlings, hoping they would come up yellow, all yellow.

Captured at Last!

It was easy. The photographers hadn't gone any farther than Imbituba. Sent back to the capital, they were being held in the city jail. The news was all over the radio and television. The papers carried front page stories. On the screen they came across as timid as rabbits. The couple hid their faces, but the assistant didn't, demonstrating to the world that he had never seen a television camera up close before. Eyes bulging, they looked more awestruck than afraid.

The Chief Investigator with the Bureau of Public Safety announced that he was taking charge of the case. The kidnappers hadn't confessed yet, but that would come in the next few hours. They didn't have the boy, and they denied everything, but, the Bureau Chief guaranteed, the case would be closed shortly. The press was not allowed to interview the suspects. "Later," the Bureau Chief said. "Later on they'll be ready to talk to the public. In the meantime, we need to conduct the interrogation without interference." Mr. Lourenço stayed in the background. Once a reporter tried to talk to him, but he wouldn't open his mouth.

To describe the commotion that overwhelmed Santo Anastácio

that day would be like describing, for example, the Holy Spirit Day festival. Without all the decorations, of course. The church stayed open all day, people were going in and out, and the vicar was elated. Many requests were made for masses to be said in thanks for the capture of the kidnappers and asking for the quick return of Claudinho—these from the more optimistic people, because the pessimistic ones were already ordering masses for the boy's soul, which the priest refused to say. He got pretty mad about it too. Whoever heard of such a thing? Who can say for certain that the boy's dead? Later on, someone did. And, incredible as it seems, it was someone who should have been the last to say so.

The First Invitation to Visit the Police Station

For three days, the prisoners were held incommunicado, at least to the press. They must have talked to the police at considerable, if not excessive, length, but unfortunately there weren't any witnesses to those cordial conversations. On the fourth day, the Chief of the Bureau of Public Safety called a press conference and made a statement that was later seen to confirm, in a way, what Mr. Lourenço had already told us.

During this period, lots of things were happening in Santo Anastácio, and I don't know if I'll be able to put down the facts in the order in which they occurred. But, at any rate, I'll write down what happened as I remember it. Also, I don't know if I'll be able to reproduce the facts as faithfully and realistically as I have up to now. It's just that, during that time, I was going around kind of dazed and confused, with terrible headaches and a fever. I think I must have caught a cold but, happily, with the medicine Tubbs gave me, I got over it. Incidentally, when I was at the drugstore, he told me what people were saying around town, and every single one had expressed sorrow, at the very least, over the fact that Claudinho hadn't been found.

According to Tubbs, Firmino was going around saying that if the police couldn't get a confession out of the criminals, he, Firmino, would be more than happy to oblige. Just leave him alone with them for half an hour and they'd spit it out, every last bit. Tubbs also told me Firmino was showing everybody his gun, his "agent of justice," and saying that this business about keeping the kidnappers in jail and putting their pictures in the paper and on television, was doing them a favor, giving them attention. The way he saw it, the only place for a criminal was six feet under with six feet of dirt on top, and all he wanted was one short hour with those dirty animals to put things right. I started to tell Tubbs that I already knew about the gun, but I decided it would complicate Firmino's life so I kept my mouth shut. Besides, I didn't feel much like talking right then. Tubbs went on to say that the best thing Firmino could do was shut up, because if Mr. Lourenço found out, he wouldn't be happy and he might make things unpleasant for Firmino.

"Are you going to tell the chief?"

"Not me," Tubbs answered, "I don't want any trouble from Firmino. He's acting screwy, running around with a gun and talking crazy. I'm going to stay out of his way."

Tubbs didn't have to talk to the Chief because before long he found out, and I think what he heard must have made it sound even worse because he sent the corporal to Firmino's shop to bring him to the police station for a little talk.

A Second Invitation to Visit the Police Station

Procópio was going around tooting his horn, bragging that he was the one who got the police to act, that he was the one who identified the criminals, that if it weren't for his courage as leader of the opposition, blowing the whistle, the kidnappers wouldn't be behind bars. Peephole didn't respond, but he did defend the attitude of the authorities and praise Mr. Lourenço. Peephole also asserted that Procópio was a leftist, which was why he devoted his entire life to picking on the government over every little thing. He was an agitator, a subversive agent on Moscow's payroll. As far as the photographers were concerned, Peephole heartily approved of their arrest, although it was due considerably more to the intelligent actions of Mr. Lourenço than to the ridiculous notions that Procópio was feeding the press. I can guarantee, however, that Peephole didn't say this all at once, but rather over a period of time, because—as everyone knows—he can never get out more than ten words at a sitting. Even at the City Council meetings he's

the prototype of verbal economy. His enemies attribute it to ignorance. Mr. Lourenço evidently found out about Procópio's boast-
ing because he sent over the soldier with a little note to drop by
the police station at his convenience.

A Third Visit to the Police Station

The vicar and the tax collector also went to the police station, of
their own free and spontaneous will. The vicar wanted to tell the
chief about what the parishioners were saying, and about the
masses that had been celebrated and ones that were planned. He
stressed how shaken the faithful were and how their religious
spirit was really coming out in these trying times. There were
vows, many prayers, the altars were filled with candles. He wanted
to consult Mr. Lourenço about the possibility of organizing a
procession—that is, if the authorities thought a big gathering
wouldn't be too great a risk at the moment, possibly inciting a riot,
for example. That agitator of a Councilman had stirred up
enough trouble already and he, the priest, didn't want to add to
the problem, but his parishioners had asked for a procession and
he still hadn't given them an answer.

The tax collector was there to pass on to Mr. Lourenço what he
had learned in the course of his duties, since he deemed it his
obligation, as an official of the state government, to cooperate with
the police in the maintenance of public order and security. The
tax collector had not observed the religious spirit the vicar reported. The majority appeared to be thinking along the lines of
violence. Most people were after the photographers' heads. Some
were going around saying they wished Brazil had the death
penalty. Others had reached the point of asserting that, if the
photographers should be moved to the police station in Santo
Anastácio, there would be no guarantee of protection. The moment would come when the whole town would rise up and take
justice into their own hands. The Chief could easily arrange an
escape attempt at a previously established time, and they would
take care of the rest.

Mr. Lourenço listened attentively and sent the vicar and the tax
collector on their way with his assurances. The procession could
be held whenever the priest wanted, but it would be better—and

he himself would join in—if it could be held after the case was over, as a festival of celebration and thanksgiving. The vicar thought that was a fine idea. As for the vigilante spirit among some of the citizens, if they were so anxious to take action, they might as well go to the capital and get something going there because their enthusiasm wouldn't be rewarded in Santo Anastácio for the simple reason that the prisoners weren't about to be moved from the city jail since there wasn't anywhere else for them to go at the moment. Santo Anastácio didn't have a jail, the police station didn't even have cells. If they wanted to shoot something, they were welcome to take aim at Santo Anastácio's stray dogs of which there were too many on the streets. The authorities would appreciate their cooperation.

A Special Visit, Not to the Police Station

The name of Elias' daughter is Cássia. Cássia, the sleeping beauty. Or rather, sleepyhead. How come she never gets a case of insomnia, not even for one night? Why didn't she ever wake up when I was prowling around in the back of the bar, hoping her bedroom window would be open, open for love?

Cássia had a girlfriend in São Francisco who had introduced her to someone there and they wrote each other letters. I liked it when she brought in her letters to mail, but I envied her correspondent. Sometimes I wanted to tear up her letters, and if they hadn't been registered mail, I would have. Cássia, sexy beauty. I knew she was trying to excite me when she lingered in the post office sticking on the stamps. She would pretend not to notice me and answer my questions in monosyllables, but I could detect a naughty smile on those full lips. Cássia, tender beauty.

She had come to the post office when I wasn't feeling well and, naturally, noticed my condition. I told her I was feeling sick, but it wasn't anything serious, I'd be fine in a little bit. "Ah . . .," she responded, and took the stamps I gave her and started pasting them on. I took my time getting her change from the drawer, trying to catch her eye. Her delicate fingers with polished nails, holding the little brush, painting the glue on the stamps.

Sweet, beloved Cássia. My head was killing me and my face was on fire. Cássia's fingers stroking my chin, measuring my fever. It's nothing, precious, I'll be all right. Cássia's compassionate eyes gazing into mine. Cássia's hand reaching for mine, caressing it lovingly. Cássia's lips brushing mine, a little shiver. Don't be afraid, darling, nobody's coming. Cássia's breasts swelling with desire. My hands covering them greedily, squeezing them, gently, at first, then impatiently. Cássia moaning with pleasure. Me, burning up. In came my mail carrier and, as usual, he didn't even say hello. I gave him a furious look. Cássia finished gluing the stamps. I began filling out the registered letter receipt.

The Interview

On the afternoon of the fourth day after the photographers' arrest, the Chief of the Bureau of Public Safety gave an interview, excerpts of which were on television that night. *The Statesman* printed the entire text the next day. I clipped the article, and here it is, faithfully transcribed:

REPORTER: Did the suspects confess, sir?

CHIEF: No, they didn't confess, for the simple reason that they had nothing to confess.

REPORTER: Are you saying they're innocent?

CHIEF: Exactly. They're innocent. I can categorically state they are innocent.

REPORTER: And the child, sir, do you have anything to report about him?

CHIEF: I'm sorry to say, no. So far, we have no confirmed leads. As you know, information is released only after it is confirmed.

REPORTER: Does that mean, sir, that you have received new information about the child?

CHIEF: Lots of it. Unfortunately, none has checked out, it's all cold.

REPORTER: Will you explain how you came to the conclusion the photographers were innocent?

CHIEF: Certainly. Their statements, obtained during a lengthy interrogation, were verified, down to the smallest detail, and since they checked out, we reached the conclusion that they had nothing whatsoever to do with the disappearance of the child. So I'm considering it a case of a runaway.

REPORTER: Can you tell us about the prisoners' statements?

CHIEF: Certainly. I'll give you a summary of the statements and our inquiries. The couple went to Imbituba and were there the whole time. We reconstructed their movements in that city and found no sign of the child being there. It's clear the couple is not involved in the case. We're satisfied with the evidence and the couple has been cleared of the charges.

REPORTER: And the photographers' assistant, who was in Santo Anastácio on the day Claudinho disappeared?

CHIEF: We conducted a thorough investigation. The fact is, the assistant was in Santo Anastácio that afternoon collecting unpaid bills. We traced his movements in detail. He returned that evening to Imbituba, alone. We even have testimony from the attendant of a gas station where he filled up.

REPORTER: In your opinion, is it possible the child could have been hidden under the seat of the van, for example?

CHIEF: We considered that possibility and conducted some studies. Claudinho could not have been kidnapped and transported in the van, among other reasons because, at the time the boy was seen in the plaza, the photographers' assistant was calling on a customer, and here's another important detail. The assistant gave the customer a lift to the highway before he drove on to Imbituba. We checked his route between the highway and when he got to Imbituba, and we're satisfied the boy wasn't with him, nor was there time for him to go back and kidnap the child, who by then must have been either in downtown Santo Anastácio or on his way out of town.

REPORTER: Where are the photographers now?

CHIEF: They were released last night quietly, to avoid problems and allow them to go back to making their living.

REPORTER: Where did they go?

CHIEF: That's their business, don't you think? And ours, of course.

REPORTER: Why are the police still interested in them?

CHIEF: It might be necessary for them to testify. Besides, their profession requires them to obtain police authorization in each town they visit, as I'm sure you can understand, since they enter people's houses. Their contact with the authorities is a guarantee of protection for them as well.

REPORTER: What would they be called to testify about?

CHIEF: We don't know that yet.

REPORTER: What can you tell us about the results of the examination of the letter from the kidnappers?

CHIEF: The tests have been completed and the results are being withheld pending completion of the investigation.

REPORTER: The letter was delivered personally by the kidnappers to the residence of Claudinho's parents. Sir, how do you explain the kidnappers' presence in the area?

CHIEF: I'm not explaining anything, you're the one who's explaining how and by whom the letter was delivered, I didn't say anything. We're still investigating.

REPORTER: One more question, sir. Do you think the kidnappers are local people or are they from somewhere else?

CHIEF: I have no comment on that.

REPORTER: Excuse me, sir, is it true the police don't have a theory about the case? You said, sir, that you believed it was a case of a runaway, but you're investigating the letter, isn't that a contradiction?

CHIEF: Official police matters are confidential for reasons of security. I have nothing more to say at this time.

I won't transcribe the remarks of the journalist nor the editorial they published, but I can guarantee beyond the shadow of a doubt that they weren't favorable to the Chief of the Bureau of Public Safety. The press insinuated that the police had no leads and were at a loss as to what to do next. The press also suggested that the kidnappers (the newspaper stuck to the theory of a kidnapping) were probably still in the capital, or at least had an accomplice there. The editorial regretted the lack of communication between the authorities and the public, and it called attention to the fact that, in the final analysis, it is the taxpayer's right to know what's going on behind closed doors, especially where the police are concerned because they, after all, are entrusted with safeguarding the security of the people, etc., etc., etc.

Some Thoughts That Came up During My Visit to the Police Station

After Firmino, Procópio, the vicar, and the tax collector paid their little visits to the police station, I decided to do the same. I stopped by there a lot anyway to have a cup of coffee with Mr. Lourenço, a habit acquired long before the Claudinho business occurred. Mr. Lourenço is a cultured person and I respect his views. I admire his levelheadedness and I always enjoyed having a chat with him.

I'd made a point of seeking out his company since I first met him, not only because I immediately became a part of the Anastasian information circuit down at the Central, but also because, to this day, I still remember a piece of advice from one of my teachers from back home, a guy with a reputation for being pretty smart. He used to spend practically the whole class telling stories, totally forgetting to cover the lesson or assign homework. He was always telling us stories about things that had happened to him, and he would listen to what we had to say and give really good advice. He used to say: "Listen, anytime you meet people who have brains and common sense, make friends, and spend as much time as possible with them. You won't have to talk, just listen and learn. Intelligence and common sense together are so rare these days they ought to be put in a museum." He also used to say: "Take advantage all you can of other people's minds, because you kids need all you can get."

The class used to die laughing when he would speak French. That would happen whenever he decided to give an oral test. He would call on one of us and bark out a question (he taught history and geography), the answer to which invariably inspired him to stroke an imaginary mustache and recite the famous French phrase: *l'ignorance c'est une chose admirable!* Since he would never give a grade below ninety on the test, I always understood the phrase to be a compliment, and later on I began to think that there must be some virtue to ignorance. One of these days I'll get around to discussing the matter with Mr. Lourenço to see what he thinks about it.

At the police station I steered the conversation around to what I wanted to find out, namely, what had happened in the earlier visits. Firmino, poor guy, had to listen to a sermon, and on top of that was relieved of his gun, which wasn't registered. Mr. Lourenço confiscated it. To make it even worse, Firmino had to confess the gun was Celina's, who herself had taken it from a client who owed her money. Since the topic of Celina came up, I was tempted to tell Mr. Lourenço about my encounter with Firmino at her house, but I decided it wasn't quite the right moment, better to wait a little. I still wasn't sure about my suspicions. Patience and chicken soup, the old folks say.

As for Procópio, Mr. Lourenço made him see that his attitude was not very thoughtful or useful. It made no difference as far as the police were concerned, because they had been keeping an eye on the suspects for a long time, and if the arrest hadn't been made earlier, it was only to avoid alarming people. Mr. Lourenço actually spoke highly of the Councilman to me, referring to his combative spirit and his courage. Mr. Lourenço said Procópio was a typical, provincial Don Quixote, faithful defender of utopian causes. I liked the description. Don Quixote is a famous character from literature, as everyone knows, even though not many people have read the book. Including me. Nevertheless, I've heard some references to his importance and to prove that I'm not only interested in detective literature, I want to make it clear here that I understood what Mr. Lourenço meant when he described Procópio that way. It's true I had to look up utopian in the dictionary.

Mr. Lourenço's Reservations

After the second cup of coffee, I took the initiative: "Mr. Lourenço, do you think the photographers really did kidnap Claudinho? And where is the boy?" He looked at me for a long time, as if he were interrogating me.

"Mr. Lourenço . . .?"

"I don't know, Jerônimo, I don't know, I have my doubts. If Claudinho was kidnapped, I'm inclined to believe it was someone else. There's very little evidence against the photographers' assistant. I don't know . . . I just don't know."

"But, why, Mr. Lourenço?"

"You really want to know? Well, okay then, I'll tell you. I think you've got the brains to understand the situation, and maybe you can help."

"Me, help you, Mr. Lourenço?"

"Why not? Sometimes we, the police, need help from the public, principally the disinterested views of an intelligent person, so . . ."

"Well, I appreciate your confidence in me, if there's anything I can do . . ."

"There is. Listen to me and then tell me if I'm right or wrong, okay? I have my doubts about the case, and I'm going to tell you what they are as they occur to me, not in any particular order. One of my reservations is this: if the boy was kidnapped, there has to be a motive, and the most logical one is money. I don't see any other, unless it's revenge, but I know Cirilo pretty well and I haven't found anything that would be cause for revenge. Therefore, it has to be money, okay? But that's where it doesn't make sense . . ."

"Why not, Mr. Lourenço?"

"Look at it this way, if money was the motive, why did they wait so long to send the ransom note? And another thing: the amount of money they demanded doesn't seem like enough. What do you think?" I admit at that moment nothing occurred to me. I hadn't thought about it that way before. The time problem didn't seem to mean much of anything, and it seemed like a reasonable amount of money to me. I think my reaction pleased Mr. Lourenço because he smiled and his eyes were shining.

"That's what I'm wondering," he went on. "If they kidnapped the boy, why would the photographers only ask for a hundred thousand cruzeiros? It doesn't make sense. I'm convinced they would demand more, something on the order of a million, at the very least."

A million! That was a lot. I wondered if my ideas made any sense? Still, I never would have imagined the motive was such a large amount of money!

Another Visit, This One Unexpected

While Mr. Lourenço and I were talking, the corporal knocked and stuck his head in the door. "Excuse me, sir, Naldo is here, the night watchman at town hall, he wants to talk to you."

"See what he wants, will you?"

"I asked, but he says he'll only talk to you."

"All right, tell him I'll be with him in a minute."

I thought I'd better leave. "Don't go, Jerônimo, this won't take long, just stay put, I haven't finished telling you my thoughts on the subject."

"Do you have an idea, then, who the kidnappers are?"

"No, I don't have any idea. What I do have, like I said, is doubts. Look, here's another thing that bothers me: Why haven't the kidnappers gotten in touch again? Have you thought about that?"

"Well, if they were the photographers, since they were in jail . . ."

"Very good, then I'll ask you this: Who put the letter under

Cirilo's door? The photographers were in Imbituba and the assistant had already returned there too . . ."

"Ah, that I don't know, Chief . . . I mean . . . who knows, maybe it was someone else?"

"Exactly, my boy, exactly, maybe it was someone else. And in that case we have two hypotheses; either the photographers had an accomplice here in Santo Anastácio, or it wasn't the photographers at all, but someone else, someone who was here the whole time or, at least, no farther away than the capital."

Word of honor, that Mr. Lourenço is one smart guy! It's never a waste of time talking to him. You learn a lot of important things! The most interesting thing is that the interview with the Chief of the Bureau of Public Safety, soon afterward, corroborated in part what Mr. Lourenço told me. And what's more: the second hypothesis fit in with what I was thinking. That's when I was going to explain it to Mr. Lourenço. I had my mouth open when he interrupted: "That's how I see it . . . but the worst thing is that we could be dealing with a . . ."

The corporal came in again. "Sir, Naldo is still waiting, should I tell him you can't see him now?"

"No, tell him to come in."

The Outline of a Figure With Jacket and Cap

Naldo's arrival was timely. It gave me an opportunity to explain clearly to Mr. Lourenço everything that was hammering at my brain. What Naldo told the Chief was this: last night, while he was on duty, he was looking out the window of the Mayor's office, counting the lights on the other side of the bay, trying to stay awake—both Mr. Lourenço and I saw right away what a lie that was because the whole town knows that Naldo sleeps on the job all the time; what's more likely is that he woke up to urinate or get a drink of water—when he noticed, about one o'clock, a figure with a sack over one shoulder, going toward the jetty. Curious, Naldo watched the figure walk to the end of the landfill and throw the sack into the water. He, Naldo, was disturbed by it, but he was too scared to go out and investigate. The figure was definitely that of a man, wearing a short jacket with the collar turned up and a cap with the ear flaps down, practically covering his face.

"Listen, Naldo," Mr. Lourenço asked, "from way back there,

with hardly any lights on in the building, are you absolutely sure you saw a man dressed like that, throwing a sack in the water? Are you sure you weren't dreaming, Naldo?"

The watchman looked offended by the chief's insinuation and insisted he had seen it, protesting that he had made a point of coming to the police station to talk personally to Mr. Lourenço, because he had the strong impression that the man was doing something wrong, something illegal.

"All right, Naldo, I appreciate your cooperation, but I'm going to have to ask you not to mention this to anyone, understand? I don't want complications. It could be something absolutely ordinary, like someone getting rid of some garbage by tossing it in our charming, filthy bay."

After Naldo left, we talked about what he had said. Mr. Lourenço didn't attach any importance to it. "Jerônimo, you know and everybody else knows that people throw things in the water all the time. Dead animals, old household junk. Our watchman was either sleepwalking or what he saw was an ordinary citizen going about his business, dumping some trash or old shoes."

I couldn't keep my idea to myself any longer: "Mr. Lourenço, did you notice Naldo's description?"

"What description?"

"The one he gave of the jacket and the cap. Don't they suggest anything to you?"

"Sure they do, they suggest the guy was cold and he bundled up to go outside in the middle of the night."

"Not that, what I mean is, don't the jacket and cap remind you of anyone?"

"Here in Santo Anastácio? Lots of people, including me."

"I don't mean you, because your cap doesn't have earflaps, I'm talking about the only person in this part of town who fits the description."

"And who might that be?"

"Well, Mr. Lourenço, don't you think it sounds like Firmino?"

The First Revelation

The evening after the interview with the Chief of the Bureau of Public Safety appeared in the newspaper, Cirilo joined us, very nervous and obviously grief-stricken, making it clear he no longer held out the slightest hope of seeing his son again. He told us about a dream he had. It went like this: an old man appeared and consoled Cirilo very kindly, encouraging him to face reality, accept the facts as they were. The old man looked like Cirilo's father, who died a few years back. In the dream, he decided to pay Cirilo a visit, seeing him so despondent. Cirilo was in an open field, under a clear bright sky, but he wasn't hot, on the contrary, a fresh breeze was blowing ("What it means is your father is a spirit of light," explained Firmino, which seemed to please Cirilo very much). The old man came toward him and embraced him, and Cirilo felt that both of them were floating in space ("That means the old man is a guide").

Then the old man spoke: "Don't cry, my son, don't cry for Claudinho, in death he is with you and yours on earth, not with us." In the dream, Cirilo embraced his father and wept copiously. "Don't cry, my son, don't cry, Claudinho is fine, he died the innocent boy he was, he's happy with the angels, let the law of man strike down those who cut that life off, sooner or later they will pay." At this point of the narration, Cirilo lost control and sniffled a little, his eyes brimming with tears.

All of us kept a respectful silence until it was broken by Firmino: "It's going to be all right, Cirilo. Look at the dream, it's a revelation, your son is a saint. What you should do now is let me take you to one of our ceremonies. You need to let the spirits speak. We'll arrange a session and find out who killed Claudinho."

Mr. Lourenço didn't say anything, but I could tell he didn't like the idea by the way he looked at Firmino. Tubbs and Peephole looked like they were at a wake, as if they were about to go over and offer Cirilo their condolences. Elias served Cirilo a generous dose of brandy and poured himself one.

After what I had told Mr. Lourenço, I was curious, very curious indeed. I wanted to know if it was possible to use dead people's dreams to find out things, like, for example, the location of someone who disappeared. Procópio, who, after his recent failure, was staying away from flights of oratorical fancy, took out a cigarette and lit it. He looked at Cirilo, then at Mr. Lourenço, and kept his mouth shut. Once bitten, twice shy.

I decided to go ahead and ask: "Cirilo, the old man . . . you mean, your dead father didn't say how Claudinho died?"

"No, unfortunately he didn't say anything about that, but then it doesn't matter much anymore how he died, I accept what the dream said. What I have to do is get used to the idea. There's only one thing I really want, and that's to find his body so we can give him a decent, Christian burial. That's what I'd like. I won't rest easy until he has a final resting place."

"Don't worry, Cirilo," said Firmino, "we'll find him, trust me. Now that we know it wasn't those swindlers like the authorities thought" (and here he gave a quick but significant glance at Mr. Lourenço), "we'll get to work, and find out what happened, I promise you."

"Look, can you explain this business to me? Is it really true that dead people can talk and reveal secrets?"

"Listen, Jerônimo," responded Firmino (Firmino himself!), "you'll find out soon enough how true it is. Cirilo's going to have another revelation, I'll bet on it, all he has to do is call the spirits, find a good group to perform the ritual . . ."

I looked at Mr. Lourenço and I think he understood me. We didn't need to exchange words for him to see how much Firmino's nerve impressed me. Before the conversation got any further, the chief stepped in: "All right, people, I respect Cirilo's dream, but, until we have a body, we can't be sure anyone's dead. Fine, let's suppose Cirilo is right. At any rate we have to go on with the investigation until the case is solved. And you, Firmino, you've been looking for an itch to scratch. I suggest you stay out of this. Now, I think that's enough talk for today. I hope Cirilo will understand, I know what he's going through, but as a police officer I simply can't accept this kind of talk . . . I know, I'm sorry, but dreams and revelations, although of course I respect other people's beliefs. Let's go get some sleep, what do you think?" Everybody agreed.

The Second Revelation, the Second Time Around

Cirilo and Firmino left together. Mr. Lourenço took my arm and we went for a walk in the cold, night air. The only sounds were our muffled footsteps and, marking a counterpoint, the intermittent barking of the dogs roaming the plaza, watering the palm trees, digging up the dirt in the gardens. "See how things are, Jerônimo, while we discuss whether dead people can or can't help find a criminal, dogs are running around ruining the municipal gardens, peeing on the trees whenever they feel like it, barking at the moon, perpetuating the species, without the slightest awareness of the cold and without discussing questions of logic or the lack thereof."

I sensed that Mr. Lourenço was laughing inside, in spite of his serious expression. The pack of mongrels started to irritate me. I looked for a stone on the ground, but I couldn't find one.

"Will you excuse me for a minute?"

"What's wrong?"

I took my arm out of Mr. Lourenço's grasp and ran toward the plaza stamping my feet hard on the ground. The hungry dogs scattered. It's terrible! Every morning the gardener had to repair the damage.

When I returned, Mr. Lourenço was laughing heartily: "Very good, my industrious caretaker, I think I'll recommend the Mayor hire you to take care of the plaza. Come on, let's walk, it's cold."

I took advantage of his good mood and brought the conversation around to Firmino. What did Mr. Lourenço think about his attitude, wasn't he being pretty insolent?

"To tell you the truth, I've been thinking a lot about what you told me and I've been considering it from various angles" (I had told the Chief about running into Firmino at Celina's, and about his relations with her and his extra expenses, from which, putting things together, I suggested the idea that he kidnapped Claudinho), "and despite the fact that I don't want to jump to conclusions, I have to accept some things. You're not in a hurry are you?"

"No." We were in front of the post office.

"Well then, let's analyze it together: first, if there was a kidnapping, the motive must be money; second, the kidnapper or kidnappers couldn't be too far from Santo Anastácio, or else they have an accomplice nearby, don't forget the letter; third, the boy disappeared from here at the plaza, but immediately following his visit to Firmino's workshop; fourth, Firmino is always trying to borrow money; fifth, Firmino supports a mistress in the red light district, which obviously represents a considerable expense for him. Up to that point, he could, of course, be a suspect."

"And there's the watchman's story too."

"That's right, but that's what I'm not happy with, because, to accept that, I have to accept that Claudinho is dead."

"But, if Firmino really is the kidnapper, as you believe . . ."

"I don't believe any such thing! You're the one who thinks so, it's your theory."

"Okay, I'm the one who got suspicious about him first. But, if it is him, ask yourself this, how could he let the kid go after getting the money? He'd be caught. I knew Claudinho, he's a bright kid. No matter how well Firmino covered his face or disguised himself, he'd be recognized, or else the accomplices, maybe even Celina, would be identified. So Firmino didn't have any choice except to kill the boy and give the whole thing up. What do you think?"

"I agree that the kidnapper, if there is one, appears to have given up. But as for killing . . . I don't know, I just don't know . . . Assuming Firmino could be a kidnapper, then I admit it fits. But to assume he's a murderer?! That's another thing altogether . . ."

On the Usefulness of My Novel

I'm exhausted. I wrote all morning and afternoon, intensely and without taking any breaks. I didn't really start the book until after the case was solved, although, like I said before, as soon as the boy disappeared, the plot was outlined in my mind. But while the events were occurring, all I did was take notes and sketch out the narrative. When everything was finally cleared up is when I started writing. Then I wrote like crazy. I didn't do anything else. I only stopped to eat and at night I'd fall in bed without even taking off my clothes. I'm worn out today and I feel like quitting. But it's almost over. A few more chapters and I'll be finished. I realize now that, if I had started writing along with the events, the first draft would already be in the hands of some editor. My mistake was to wait until the end to get the story going. My notes and outlines helped me maintain a certain order in the plot, but I wasted a lot of time with them, rereading and revising them.

All of this comes to mind right now because it was on a similar occasion, when I was sitting at the typewriter at my desk, exhausted, that Mr. Lourenço arrived at the post office and sat down in front of me. I think it was the day after our conversation in the plaza. He asked me what I was typing.

"It's nothing much, just some notes."

"About what, Jerônimo?"

"I guess I already told you that I always liked to write. Well, I decided to take notes about what's happening here because, I confess, Mr. Lourenço, it's inspired me to write a detective novel. I think it's my big chance."

Mr. Lourenço was really interested and said he was impressed by what I was doing. "You know, Jerônimo, besides your literary project, these notes could help me a lot. What a good thing I dropped by."

I can't deny that I was flattered. I wanted to know how my notes could help.

"Very easy . . . if you have everything written down there, I can study them analytically as part of my investigation. That's why I'm going to ask if you'll do me a favor. Will you lend me your notes? I can get them back to you in a couple of days."

I didn't hesitate. I gave him the pages in my drawer. Mr. Lourenço looked at them carefully, examining each one.

"Jerônimo, you're a very organized young man. You can't imagine how this is going to help me. These are fine notes. I'm going to read them with the care that they deserve and then I'll return them. This is exactly what I needed to reconstruct the events. I really appreciate it."

I accompanied him to the door and watched as he walked away. He passed the police station and disappeared behind the church. Why was he going to Firmino's shop?

More Praise for My Person

The next afternoon, Mr. Lourenço returned the typed pages. He thanked me again, and made a point of saying that they had been very useful to him.

"You know, Jerônimo, reading your notes gave me a chance to go over everything, get it all straight in this poor old head of mine . . . at my age, you start forgetting things. If it's not written down, it might as well be dead and buried. You taught me an important lesson. Who would have guessed that the Police Chief himself needed to have the case explained to him. But fortunately I found an excellent assistant."

I think I blushed at praise like that coming from a man as intelligent as Mr. Lourenço.

"Look, I'm not an expert on literature, and I don't know much about it except what I like, what I get off on, as the young people say, but I can guarantee one thing, if you manage to make these notes into a novel, I think it'll be a good one. The action is all right there, all you have to do is find the words. Who knows, maybe you'll end up being a Brazilian Edgar Wallace."

Mr. Lourenço's words were a tremendous inspiration to me. Right then and there, I made up my mind not to give up. Like the chief said, maybe I'll turn out to be a great writer, and all over the country people will know my name. Ah! It hurt me, though, that fateful afternoon, to think that one person's loss is another's gain, because I foresaw that Claudinho's misfortune would be the start of my good fortune.

"Thank you, Mr. Lourenço," was all I managed to say. I put the pages back in the drawer without looking at them.

The Red Truck

I saw Mr. Lourenço to the door. The threatening weather was fulfilling its promise. A light rain was falling, blowing in from the south. The bay was half-hidden by a fine damp curtain. The plaza was empty. Not even the dogs were out. There was a biting chill in the air that made one want to go home and curl up with a good detective novel. Mr. Lourenço didn't make a move to leave. I took advantage of the situation: "Mr. Lourenço, could you tell me why you went to Firmino's shop yesterday?"

He looked at me as if he had expected the question. He smiled.

"That's right, I almost forgot, you certainly have earned the right to know (I lowered my eyes, modestly). I went to Firmino's to check out the possibility that he was the man Naldo saw, although I still don't think there's anything to that story, as I said before. But we can't afford to overlook any piece of information, that's the way it goes in this business."

"What did you find out?"

"Nothing, not a thing."

When I tried to get more out of him, I was startled by the appearance of a red truck that came speeding around the plaza and stopped in front of the police station. It was from the Fire fighters' Search and Rescue Unit.

"What's that? Look, they stopped in front of the . . ."

"I know, I called them. Come on, let's go. I think we're finally going to come up with some solid evidence."

Despite the rain, people were coming out of the woodwork to watch. Tubbs was one of the first. He stood observing from the door of the drugstore.

An Intriguing Discovery

I feel weak. I don't know if I can go on. I think I've overdone it. I worked after dinner yesterday too. I was writing until late, I didn't look at the clock. When I couldn't see straight anymore, I fell into bed. Reading over the pages I've typed—and there are lots of them now—I see that I can't quit. I'm almost at the end. I sense it. I'm certain. One more push and the book will be done. There's not much left, just the climax and what happens after that. I don't know if I'll have the strength to finish. Yesterday I had a horrible headache. I couldn't sleep and my legs wouldn't relax, they kept twitching and jerking in little spasms under the covers. My burning eyes were open and, in the dark room, along with the familiar things I knew all too well, I could see grotesque figures flickering on the wall: gray, silent movies, the same scenes played over and over.

I feel weak. My mind is fuzzy, and my memory comes and goes. I sit at the typewriter for the longest time, and my thoughts go off in the strangest directions.

Mr. Lourenço stroking his mustache although he doesn't have one, and saying: *l'ignorance c'est une chose admirable.*

Firmino pointing the gun at Celina, naked, sitting on my lap. I throw the two of us on the floor, the gun fires at the empty chair.

An old man with a long white beard, a heavy sack over his shoulder, is consoling me: don't cry, my son, don't cry, life is a neverending struggle.

Cássia looking at some stamps spread out on the table, running her fingers through Claudinho's hair, kissing his forehead, pulling his head toward her breasts, holding it in her naked arms: I don't love you anymore Jerônimo, now that I have my son to love.

Claudinho disappears, leaving Cássia holding a wisp of smoke. Then she offers me her lips, whispers my name, I throw myself on her with unrestrained fury, embracing her with hate, she moans and screams: No! I shove her away and hit her in the head, hard, again and again, harder and harder, until an amorphous, wet gelatinous mass, stinging like a jelly fish, slowly covers me.

I have to refer to my notes all the time to organize my ideas. Looking them over, I realize now that a page is missing. I can't have lost it. They were here all the time, in the manila folder. But I'm positive a page is missing. The page where I wrote down the details of the story that Naldo told the chief. It doesn't really matter, since that chapter is already written, but it's odd. I wonder where it went? It was typed up and everything.

Gone Fishing

I told my mail carrier not to leave the post office and I left with Mr. Lourenço. He explained to the foreman of the fire fighters crew that he wanted the area around the jetty searched for a sack. Did they have the equipment?

"You bet, it's all here. What are we looking for, a body?"

"I don't know, sergeant, I don't know, maybe so, maybe not, maybe we'll find a whole lot of old shoes."

The sergeant went over to the truck and gave the order. Following the sergeant to the water was a procession led by the Chief, who was talking to me about his eternal doubts. Tubbs had a child's umbrella that barely covered him, and he was trying to hold it over the tax collector too, who was stumbling along, tripping over his own feet. Firmino followed behind them, wearing his cap and jacket. The rest scurried along, mostly in pairs, with raincoats or coats with the collars turned up, hats or caps pulled down low over their eyes, half a dozen umbrellas with water pouring off, pausing now and then for their companions to catch up. The truck was leading the way, a hearse without flowers or wreaths, a gaudy blood red. In the back of the truck was a rowboat covered with a tarp. Four men were seated around it. It looked like a casket waiting for a corpse.

They stopped. The fire fighters took the boat out and put it in the water. One man rowed while the other dragged the bottom with a long rope with hooks on the end. Two more fire fighters were on the jetty casting their ropes along the rocks at the edge and pulling them in hard in a regular back and forth motion, watched by many curious eyes. The oilcloth caps of the fire fighters looked like black glass. Mr. Lourenço was staring at the water, as if he wanted to see through it. As more people arrived, explanations and comments circulated through the crowd.

"Mr. Lourenço," I asked, "does this mean that you think the sack Firmino threw in . . ."

He cut me off: "Hold on there, Jerônimo, I don't know if Firmino threw anything in the water, nor if what Naldo said is true. We're fishing, that's all."

"But you said this time we'd find some real evidence."

"We might, but then again, we might not. Who knows what we'll find. Do you have anything special in mind?"

"Well, you know about my suspicions."

He took my arm, as he often did when he wanted to make a point, and we strolled away from the crowd. "All right, Jerônimo, I'll tell you it was because of your theory that I arranged for the search. Let's suppose that someone . . ."

"You mean Firmino?"

". . . I don't know who, that someone actually did throw a sack in the water. It might not mean anything, or it might mean what you and I both think, right?"

"Of course, I agree, but I think that the guy Naldo saw has to be Firmino."

"That's another story, what I want to find out now is if there's a sack in there and what's in it. That's all I'm concerned about at the moment."

While we were walking back to the edge of the water, the fire fighter who was in the boat throwing out the line, shouted: "Over here, sergeant, I found something!"

He pulled the line in slowly. Attached to the hook was a sack which looked to me, from a distance, like it was made of burlap and fairly small.

The Result of the Fishing Expedition

The boat came in through the rough water and beached. The crowd ran to meet it. People standing on the jetty jumped down, falling to their knees, sinking into the soft sand. The rain had let

up. A sea breeze was blowing the dark clouds away to the north.
Mr. Lourenço shouted to the crowd to keep back from the sack
which the fire fighters had placed on the sand. The sergeant and
the other military police tried to clear the area, pushing the most
enthusiastic spectators back. The Mayor attempted to make a
speech but was cut short by a curt gesture from the Chief. The
Mayor's first words—"Ladies and gentlemen, innocence de-
filed"—were carried off by the wind, lost in the clouds, taken far,
far away where they could do no harm to the weary ears of the
townspeople.

Mr. Lourenço bent down next to the sack, which had been tied
tightly at the top and attached to a medium-sized rock. He mut-
tered something, looked around, and said: "Move farther back,
please."

The circle grudgingly backed up. Mr. Lourenço stood up and
gave the order to the corporal: "Open it."

The two fire fighters on the jetty were still dragging the rocks,
since the sergeant hadn't given the order to quit. Mr. Lourenço's
eyes picked me out in the crowd, and I understood what he was
saying: so we finally have something concrete. Do you think this is
it?

I responded with a look: I think the sack's a little small, don't
you?

The corporal cut the rope. Firmino, who had stayed at the back
of the crowd, pushed through and went over to Mr. Lourenço.
The corporal made a slice through the cloth that was already
somewhat torn, and finished the job by ripping it open with his
hands. The contents were exposed. Mr. Lourenço looked at Firmino. So did I. I confess, I was surprised.

It was a pillowcase of indefinite color, with another rock tied to
the top. There was something inside, but it was hard to tell what
by the shape. Firmino tried to say something to the chief, but he
gave a sign to be quiet. The corporal proceeded with the pillowcase in the same way he had with the sack. There was some
noise from the crowd when the soggy, decomposing, stewed body
emerged. The other little bodies, in identical condition, were
huddled around the mother, as if they were still anxious for a last
turn at the white, swollen teat. The crowd broke up, talking and
joking. Firmino went over to the chief: "It's just like I told you."

"I know, Firmino, I know. It's all right, I had to do it."

I didn't say anything and Mr. Lourenço didn't say anything to me. It wasn't necessary. The three of us walked quickly away, as if we were trying to escape from something.

The corporal asked: "What do I do with the cats, Mr. Lourenço?"

"Bury them, my friend, bury them."

Macabre Correspondence

Most of the people left. The spectators looking out the windows of town hall went back to work. There was hardly anyone left on the jetty. The two fire fighters kept on dragging the rocks, as if nothing had happened. The sergeant wanted to know if they could quit, but Mr. Lourenço didn't answer.

We were walking, with Mr. Lourenço between Firmino and me, toward the water's edge. Tubbs was following a little behind, still accompanied by the tax collector. I glanced behind me and saw that the guys from the Central were all there. Except for Cirilo. Elias, Peephole, and Procópio were faithfully waiting, as if they were expecting some order or decision.

Mr. Lourenço spoke, more to himself than to us: "Well, it's just like I thought." And to me: "So, Jerônimo, where do we go from here?"

I didn't have time to respond. One of the fire fighters diverted our attention: "Hey sergeant, give me a hand here, I think I got something."

We practically ran over to the fire fighter who was pulling fairly hard on the line. The sergeant and another fire fighter went over to help. With some effort they removed the hooks. This time the Chief didn't have to give orders. The sergeant himself yelled at the driver to bring some pliers. The sack was tied shut with copper wire. Close up, I saw it was a canvas sack, fairly big and heavy. Besides a body, it probably contained some other object, like rocks. Old iron weights, I thought.

"So Jerônimo, it looks like it's finally over." Mr. Lourenço, in his usual manner, politely took my arm and asked: "Did you notice what kind of sack it is?"

Yes, I noticed. Even though it was faded, it still showed traces of the green and yellow vertical stripes and the logo of the postal service.

"Macabre correspondence, wouldn't you say, Jerônimo?"

I didn't answer. I knew as well as he, as well as the others, what Mr. Lourenço meant.

"Let's go, my boy, come on, we have a lot to talk about. Honestly, if it hadn't been for you, we might never have figured it out."

"Me, Mr. Lourenço? You really think I helped?"

On the way to the police station, he explained it to me: "No kidding, you helped a lot. Don't you remember our discussions, your theories? Most of all, those pages you typed up? They told me who wrote the letter, Jerônimo, and from there . . . You see how much you helped me, son? Come on, I'm taking you to the capital. I think you can write your novel in peace now."

Mr. Lourenço was always such a great guy. And a good friend. And very intelligent.

Period

I'm beginning to suspect my book isn't going to end the way it should. I feel lost in the tangle of events at the end. It doesn't do any good now to consult my notes. It must be because I'm tired. I realize I've been writing like a man possessed these past days. I'm not even sure how long I've been working at it. Days? Weeks? Months? Oh, hell, have I lost track of time? Things got confusing after they fished poor Claudinho out of the bay. Very confusing. And disturbing.

I have the impression that people who don't have anything to do with the story started sticking their noses in, giving opinions, asking questions. I have the impression that I spent a fair amount of time with them, that I talked a lot and they got me all mixed up. That's the impression I have. Nothing is clear anymore, except I know I'm here in the clinic in the big house that used to belong to Dr. Eugênio, who's a Congressman now and lives in Brasília. I know that for sure and I know a lot about the clinic. I can even tell that today must be Sunday. Or a holiday. There's no doctor on duty. Just a nurse and the telephone operator. And they're off together somewhere. They think I don't know what they're up to! As if I didn't recognize that type.

Something else I know is that the soldier who always stays with me disappeared yesterday. Or was it the day before yesterday? The place is deserted. Total silence. What time is it? Everyone must be asleep. I think it's getting pretty late. I'm tired, but I'm not sleepy. I wonder if I'll make it to the end of my book? After all that, just when everything was going so well.

What's that? There's somebody in the hall. At this time of night? I wonder who it is? Oh, well hey, guys, it's you, it's the gang, this is great, I swear I was starting to miss you guys. Mr. Lourenço didn't come? And where are the others, Firmino? Just you, Elias, and Tubbs? Hey, Firmino, what are you doing with that gun? What? My god . . . no . . .

The Man under the Ceiba Tree

ARNALDO CORREA

The dead man was lying on his back, eyes open, as if he were staring at the very top of the ceiba tree. He was wearing a gray workshirt and bluejeans. Both were new, but had apparently been worn for several days, judging by the soiled condition of the pants' pockets and shirt collar.

The man was about twenty-five years old, with straight, brown hair that fell over his forehead. He had a delicate, long nose, thin lips, and a pointed chin. A prominent Adam's apple completed the angular look of his face. He was of medium build, a little on the short side. His arms lay on either side of his body, which was twisted a little to the left. If it weren't for the ugly, red stain in the middle of his chest, he might be taking a nap, with his eyes strangely open.

The Lieutenant leaned over to examine the wound. There was little blood where the knife had cut neatly through the shirt at the base of the sternum. The body was resting on one of the thick roots of the ceiba, and a small area of the man's back was exposed. On the ground, near the tree root, there was a large bloodstain, indicating the blade had gone all the way through the chest and the blood had drained out the other side.

"The knife must have entered with extraordinary force," the police officer thought. With the help of a small stick, he tried to establish the trajectory of the blade. It had entered from above. The young Lieutenant sat down on the ground, thinking: "The position of the wound indicates that the victim was attacked from the front, by someone who was very strong and taller than the victim; the killer must have pulled the knife suddenly from behind his back, catching the victim by surprise. Death had been instantaneous. There was no time for the victim to react."

The violence of the blow must have determined the position in

148

which the victim fell; backwards. The left leg, slightly bent, seemed to indicate that the body turned a little as it fell.

"This is important. The twist to the left might mean the killer is left-handed." But Rafael Quintero, Lieutenant of the Manzanillo Police, who was facing his first murder case, immediately tried to restrain the impulse to jump to conclusions. He wanted to be attentive to every detail, but mentally warned himself not to get carried away with deductions based on little or no evidence.

He looked at the victim's feet: the man had been wearing a very old pair of cowboy boots with buckles that were still shiny. At one time it must have been a good pair of boots. The legs and sockless feet inside seemed disproportionately thin. One could see several inches of flesh on the left leg, which was slightly bent. A multitude of scars on the exposed part of the leg caught the Lieutenant's attention. Carefully, he lifted the pant leg a little more and paused to consider: those scratch marks had to come from running through thicket, from chasing someone or being chased through the thorns, brambles and other types of jungle reeds that leave hundreds of small cuts in the skin.

Quintero tested the man's temperature and felt the dampness of his clothing. There was no doubt he had died during the night, lying exposed to the cold and the early morning dew of the mountains. The Lieutenant searched the pockets, being careful not to alter the position of the body, since it still had to be examined by the pathologist. Quintero found a leather billfold, a handkerchief, a comb, and a key. In the billfold were forty-one pesos, an ID from the Ministry of Public Works in the name of Alberto García, and a photo of a woman holding a baby in her arms.

"What do you know about the man?" the Lieutenant asked the engineer, who had stayed back a few steps, looking on with curiosity.

"Like I explained in Manzanillo, he showed up at the site three days ago, along with another steamroller operator; I asked to borrow them from the *compañero* who's building the irrigation system. Nobody knew them here, as far as I know."

"Did he have any visitors?"

"No, nobody's been here . . . It's pretty out of the way and we'd notice if anybody came. I'm here all the time and I always know if we have a visitor."

"And at night? . . . Couldn't he have gone out with some woman from around here?"

"I don't think so, Lieutenant . . . there aren't any houses nearby, since it's not good land. The first sugar mills are too far to walk to, you have to take a car. Here in the camp there's not much to do: you can watch TV, play dominoes, sleep . . . A few men go hiking now and then."

"Well, the thing to do now is see what else the man had with him and talk to his work partner."

Quintero signalled to an older police officer, the one who had driven the jeep in from Manzanillo, to stay and guard the body. Then Quintero and the engineer, who was in charge of the construction project, set off on foot for the camp that was about sixty meters from the ceiba.

An inspection of the few possessions of the man under the ceiba turned up no new clues. Inside his wooden suitcase, equipped with a small padlock which Quintero unlocked with the key found in the dead man's pocket, there was only clothing and an enlargement of the same photograph that was in the wallet. The police officer studied the photo, which had been taken in front of a thatched palm hut and showed, in the background, the tops of some hills.

"Yesterday he burned a bunch of stuff."

Quintero turned and looked over his right shoulder. He saw an old man with a broom in his hand.

"I clean up here," said the old man, in response to the Lieutenant's questioning gaze. "Look, over there. He burned some papers and things."

"Did you see him talking to anyone?"

"No, he kept to himself . . . He never talked to anybody."

The old man went back to his slow, methodical sweeping, effectively ending the conversation.

Quintero set up headquarters in the small office of the boss at the site who gave him a few pencils and a pad of paper. Then the Lieutenant sent for Santiago Acuña, the work partner of the man under the ceiba. Acuña was tall and strong. "The same build as the murderer," Quintero thought.

The interview with Acuña provided several interesting details:

"He moved here from back east after Hurricane Flora. A lot of construction sites were starting around here and a lot of work crews came. That was back around '64, a couple of years ago. I met him at the Gilberto dam. I'm from Palma. I got a job there and he's the one who took turns with me on the bulldozer. He did the night shift. He always liked the night shift. Then he'd sleep all day. Until we started to work with the steamroller and that's almost always day work. We got along well, I liked to work with him. Anytime I needed him to take my shift, he'd do it. I would have done the same for him too, only he never went anywhere. I never saw him with a woman, not even in Santiago for Carnival, and that's saying a lot. He used to send his whole paycheck to his family."

"Where did they live?"

"I think it was somewhere around Sancti Spíritus. He told me once he had a kid there, but he never went to see him the whole time we were together."

"Why did you come to this site?"

"They gave us a couple of changes of clothes and sent us over here. The truth is I didn't really want to because this is the sticks. The irrigation site is just outside Manzanillo and you can go into town once in a while."

"Did he know anyone here?"

"No, not as far as I know . . ."

Acuña looked thoughtful and then he added: "Now that you mention it, I remember that ever since we got here he acted strange, kind of nervous and quieter than usual. I put it down to the move. He even told me he was going back home, but I didn't pay any attention. Sometimes he'd get that way and then it would pass."

The Lieutenant knew that the cordial tone of the conversation would break down as soon as he resumed his questioning. He hesitated, but finally made up his mind to ask the inevitable question.

"Where were you last night? When was the last time you saw him?"

The effect was instantaneous. Acuña seemed to realize suddenly that he was the principal suspect in a murder investigation. His manner became stiff and guarded. "Yesterday, when my shift ended, I took a shower and ate dinner. Then I watched TV until 8:30, played dominoes until 10:00, went to the bathroom and then to bed. I have witnesses for everything."

"When was the last time you saw . . .?"

"At dinner. We ate together and after that I didn't see him again. I thought he had gone to bed early."

"Was Alberto García committed to the revolution? Was he in the militia?"

"I never heard him talk about politics. I don't think he was in the militia."

"Are you in the militia?"

"I haven't had time, Lieutenant. I'm always going from one job to another."

"All right, that's all for now."

Quintero paused briefly to consider the problem. There were seventy-six workers at the dam, thirty-two of whom lived in two small towns nearby. They were transported to the worksite every day between 6:00 and 7:00 A.M. and returned between 5:00 and 6:00 P.M. He decided this group could be eliminated from the list of suspects. That left forty-four. The murderer was certainly one of these. Quintero made up his mind to question each one of them personally.

The pathologist arrived at 11:00 A.M. and gave the Lieutenant a brief preliminary report which confirmed his earlier observations and added an important detail: the man had died between 8:00 and 11:00 P.M.

The questioning of the personnel at the site lasted until 6:00 P.M. Everyone's whereabouts seemed to be straightforward and everyone had a lot of witnesses to prove it. Most of them had stayed in the dining room watching TV. The rest had played dominoes or watched the others play. One by one, the men had gone off to bed. Most were in bed by 10:30 when the electric generator shut down. Six men, in pairs, did guard duty at the workshop, the quarry and the dam wall, places where most of the equipment was stored. Finally, two men had gone to Manzanillo after dinner. They had returned the following morning.

After eating, Quintero stayed to watch the newscast on TV. He sensed that his presence disturbed the men and that they were quieter than usual. Afterwards he watched a game of dominoes and took a walk around the camp.

Finally he went to check on the guard posts. On the way back, just before reaching the camp, he turned and walked back to the ceiba. He positioned himself approximately at the place where

Alberto García had fallen, perhaps at that very hour, the night before. It was then that he realized something odd: Alberto had fallen with his back to the camp.

Once again, Quintero went through the dining room and the dormitories to his office where he had left his notes. He decided that any one of the men could easily have left for a few minutes, gone to the ceiba, committed the murder, and returned, without anyone particularly noticing his absence.

The next day, the first rays of sun caught Quintero waiting in line for coffee. It was cold. He had slept on a cot, along with the workers, and had woken several times during the night, registering the sounds of the place: men snoring, the changing of the guards at 12:00 and 3:00, the inevitable roosters crowing.

Quintero's thoughts turned to the detective novels he had read. He couldn't recall any of those heroes in a situation like this. Just then, he was handed a mug of coffee. It was delicious. It occurred to Quintero that those other detectives didn't know what they were missing.

Passing by the ceiba, on his way back to Manzanillo, Quintero thought about how death had become something mundane for him ever since he had joined Che's troops at Caballete de Casa in 1958. But, up to now, death and its cause had always gone hand in hand, they were inseparable. Things were different now, and it seemed to Quintero that from now on this is how it would be. The struggle was growing more complicated every day, and it was becoming increasingly difficult to identify the enemy.

The forensic report was waiting for him at the office. The autopsy revealed that the man under the ceiba had suffered an injury to the abdomen three or four years ago and that the wound had healed without medical attention. The projectile had only penetrated muscular and adipose tissues, which showed entrance and exit scars. The rest of the report described the fatal wound and other details of less interest.

Quintero sat down to type up his report with two fingers. This was the part of his job that he hated but he had learned that it was extremely important to write everything down and not rely on memory for anything. His report concluded with the following:

1. The murdered man was apparently a former counterrevolutionary insurgent from Escambray. The evidence for this is: multiple scars

on the legs, a three- or four-year-old gunshot wound in the abdomen, healed over without medical attention, strange behavior including avoiding contact with the other men at the site. In addition, the victim is from the vicinity of Sancti Spíritus, and has not visited his family for two years.

2. The victim apparently went to meet someone he trusted under the ceiba. This explains the absence of any signs of struggle. The victim must have been taken totally by surprise.

3. The murderer must have had previous relations of a criminal nature with the victim which would account for the time and place of the meeting and probably the motive of the crime. There are no other apparent motives.

4. The murderer is a very strong man, taller than the victim, probably left-handed. This can be deduced from the wound, its position, and the manner in which the body fell.

5. The killer is probably one of the men who spent the night of the murder at the dam.

Recommendation

Due to the nature of the crime, pass the case on to the Department of State Security.

Quintero read over the report, correcting a few errors by hand, and left it in the Chief's office. Then he went to work on other matters. At lunch time he received a message requesting him to be available at 3:30 in the afternoon to discuss his report with Captain Alvarez, his immediate superior.

He didn't think it necessary to be punctual for the meeting with Alvarez. Their friendship ran deep. It had been forged in the years of struggle in the Sierra and in the cleanup of Escambray. When Alvarez had been chosen Chief of the Manzanillo Police, he had asked Quintero to join him there.

Quintero was surprised to find Captain Blanco and Romelio in Alvarez' office. Blanco was the representative of the Internal Affairs Ministry in Manzanillo and Romelio was head of the Department of State Security in the region. Both listened attentively as Alvarez read the report. He broke off briefly to shoot Quintero a dirty look when he arrived late, and then continued reading. When Alvarez finished with the recommendation to pass the case on to State Security, Blanco exclaimed:

"Shit! You're pretty quick to get rid of a case, aren't you!" But he spoke in a light tone and, with a gesture, invited Romelio to speak.

"We've been working on the case since yesterday, when we heard the news. Since this is one of the most important construction projects in the region, we keep a close watch on everything that goes on there. The truth is, for some time we've had serious concerns about what's happening at the site, or, to be more accurate, *about what doesn't happen.* Let me explain: There are four sites with similar characteristics in the region; at each of them, except the dam, minor acts of sabotage have occurred. To be exact, twenty-eight in the last two years. This isn't uncommon in construction, where there's a high turnover of personnel and the work area is quite large. It's not like a factory or other places where the personnel is more stable, hiring is more selective and the work area is easier to monitor."

"These acts of sabotage are characteristically carried out by one individual, at the most two or three people, and generally involve damage to equipment, small fires, etc. Each time one of these incidents occurs, we take a look at the personnel and, with the information we have about each site, it's relatively easy to identify the culprits."

"We've been wondering why, at the dam, none of this type of thing happens. The personnel is no different from that at the other sites: the only reasonable explanation is that the counter-revolution is well-organized there and under the direction of a central organization. The important thing is that we're almost certain they're planning something big. They know that if a minor act of sabotage occurs, we take action against anyone with a record, and they want to avoid that."

"But now they've let the cat out of the bag," said Alvarez.

"I think it's a risk they were forced to take."

"I'm inclined to think that Alberto García, or whatever his real name is, arrived at the site and recognized someone very important there: they were left with only two options, eliminate him or involve him. It's possible they tried to recruit the man under the ceiba and he refused. But that's not important. I suggest we continue investigating through the police, as we've done so far, normally; as if it were an ordinary case, while establishing the proper coordination between the two departments."

There was a silence. Then Blanco put his cap on and stood up, adjusting his belt with the pistol, in a clear sign that he agreed. He gave a quick salute and left. Alvarez followed, leaving Quintero behind with Romelio.

Quintero took time to study the young man facing him. The Lieutenant knew something about Romelio and admired him. It was the first time they had been alone together. Romelio had been a member of the underground resistance in Santiago de Cuba and on one occasion had been brutally tortured. His small and apparently delicate frame concealed an iron will within.

"I've brought the files of seven men who worked at the dam and who have records of collaboration with the Batista regime or of counterrevolutionary activities. We have them under surveillance and we think they're up to something, but we haven't the slightest idea what. I know none of them is the boss. Someone very clever runs the operation, from the dam itself or from outside. One of them works in the personnel department and through him they control hiring. They seem to know the backgrounds of everyone at the site down to the last detail. These seven are excellent workers. They've earned the approval of the administration and the party, another sign that they're under strict control. At other places where they've worked, almost all of them were troublemakers; but at the dam, as if by magic, they turn into model citizens."

"Where do you think I ought to go from here with the investigation?" Quintero asked. Romelio smiled and responded:

"You're asking me? I think you've done a great job. It's your case. I'm only here to help, so you tell me what to do!"

Quintero blushed. He picked up the files Romelio had given him and said:

"I think the most important thing right now is to identify the man under the ceiba."

"We've already sent the data to Havana. I expect to have an answer later today or tomorrow."

Romelio left and Quintero set to work organizing the elements of the case that had now been established.

Starting with the assumption that the crime was connected to the counterrevolution, he made a list beginning with the most politically trustworthy of the personnel. Next, he wrote down the names of the seven that Romelio had brought to his attention, and finally the rest of the personnel. Next to each name he jotted down a synthesis of the man's deposition and the names of the men who corroborated the testimony.

Going over the declarations, Quintero came upon an interesting fact, one that he hadn't noticed at first: of the seven suspects, six had spent the night at the camp. The seventh was Nivaldo Cáceres, the driver for the foreman at the dam wall, Ramón. These two had gone to Manzanillo. The depositions of the remaining six were much longer and more detailed than those of the rest of the personnel. Each of the six could account for every minute of the time. Their witnesses were precisely the most politically trustworthy of the personnel. The alibis were too good! They must have known what was going to happen that night. That's why they had been so careful to document their movements.

A few hours later, Quintero received a message from Romelio saying he had heard from Havana. Quintero joined Romelio in his office. The note read: "Identity of Alberto García: Gustavo Amengual, La Sierrita, Escambray, 1935. Joined the Pescador gang in 1963. Has been seen since with Lucio Benavides. Amengual presumed dead when Lucio's gang was captured in May 1964."

"I remember that well," said Quintero. "I was in on that chase. Fate has its ways of catching up with you."

Romelio took a coffee thermos out of a drawer in his desk and offered Quintero a cup, smiling, but silent.

For the next few days, Quintero worked feverishly, accumulating a great deal of information. But he didn't get any farther than he was on the second day of the case. He ran an exhaustive check on the six suspects' depositions, which proved to be accurate down to the last detail, in contrast to the majority of the depositions in which there were small contradictions and a few gaps. But aside from his intuition, Quintero had nothing concrete to go on, and he was beginning to get frustrated.

He decided to tell Romelio he was thinking of giving up. Quintero knew that the best time to talk to Romelio was after ten at night. Quintero found him listening to music and studying a math book. Romelio took the thermos out of the drawer and, after serving his visitor a cup of steaming coffee, poured some for himself.

"I'm sorry, Romelio, but I'm at a dead end and I'm about ready to quit. I thought the case was going to be easier. When I saw the guy's legs, I knew he was an insurgent. When it turned out he was, I decided I must be a great detective. But for two weeks now I've been working morning, noon and night on the case and I haven't even earned my keep."

"Don't get discouraged. We're on the right track. Why don't we think this through from the beginning? Maybe we'll find something we missed. Look, you start at the beginning and tell me about the case as if I didn't know a thing about it."

Quintero looked skeptical, but decided to go along with the experiment.

"All the evidence indicates that Amengual was killed by someone he knew from back when he was an insurgent in Escambray. Apparently, they ran into each other at the site. It's possible they tried to recruit Amengual, or they simply decided he was too dangerous because he knew the killer's real identity. Amengual also was extremely interested in keeping his identity a secret. The two arrange to meet. The killer watches TV or plays dominoes. At an opportune moment, he slips out, saying he's going to the latrine. Making sure no one has seen him, he then heads for the ceiba where he kills Amengual. He returns, having hidden the weapon; perhaps he had dug a hole earlier in order to bury the knife. Then, like someone returning from the john, he rejoins the group. His absence has not been noted. You see then, it's a perfect crime. Forty-two suspects, each one with a good alibi. It's a dead end."

"Wait a minute, slow down now. Let's start with his activities in Escambray, which is where the story really begins. Alberto García, actually Gustavo Amengual, joins el Pescador's band of insurgents and they're wiped out."

"I remember that one managed to escape through some caves, so it must have been him."

"Afterwards he joins Lucio Benavides' gang, where he must have met his future killer."

"I was in on that operation. There were twelve in all. We killed eight and took two prisoners. One guy they called el Gordo managed to escape, we don't know how. Eventually, we assumed the other one died. The prisoners told us they had seen him lying with a bullet in his stomach. We went to the place they told us they had seen him and we found a trail of blood that ended at the Agabama. We figured the body had been washed down the river.

In reality, Amengual must have survived, only to end up dying here, under the ceiba, with the name Alberto García."

"So, if we're right, el Gordo must have killed him."

"That's it!"

"It all makes sense now. El Gordo comes here, takes control of the counterrevolution and plans a major attack. Like a ghost from the past, Amengual, who's supposed to be dead, shows up. Until then, El Gordo thinks he's safe: with Lucio and his gang eliminated, the prisoners convicted and shot, nobody knows about his past. He decides to kill Amengual, who has probably refused to participate again in this kind of activity. But I doubt such a clever man would take a chance on being seen returning from the ceiba or lurking around behind the latrine. It doesn't fit his personality." Quintero had to admit what Romelio said made sense, but he insisted:

"There are seventy-six men on the job. We have to assume it was someone on the inside."

"Exactly!"

"I think we can eliminate the thirty-two workers who live at the sugar mill. They left early."

"For the time being, okay, we'll eliminate them."

"So we're back to the same story. We have to discount the two men who went to Manzanillo, so that leaves forty-two in the camp. One of them has to be the killer."

"Why exclude the two who went to Manzanillo?"

Quintero looked thoughtful. Romelio went on.

"They could have reached the highway, waited there, and then come back. Who are they?"

"Ramón, the foreman at the dam, and his driver."

"The driver's name is Nivaldo Cáceres, alias the Rat. He's on the list I gave you."

"I think you've hit the nail on the head! I just remembered something else: the victim fell with his back turned to the camp, as if the killer had come from the road."

The dam site is nothing but a dirty yellow patch in the blue hills. One day it will be a great lake of crystalline water. A jeep wound around the embankment that runs into the dam two kilometers away. When Quintero arrived, he set up shop in the office of the chief engineer, and Romelio settled in the warehouse. Quintero gave orders to pick up six men.

Quintero asked the chief engineer to send in Nivaldo Cáceres, the driver for the foreman, Ramón. Nivaldo looked pale and uneasy. It was then that Quintero noticed that sometimes people's names fit them exactly. Nivaldo looked just like a rat.

Quintero removed his holster and pistol with studied ease and hung them on a nail near the window that looked out over the ceiba. Then he sat down in a chair behind the small desk.

"You know why I sent for you? No? In your declaration here there are a few points I'd like to clarify."

Nivaldo looked relieved.

"What time did you reach Manzanillo?"

"I don't have a watch, but I guess it was about ten at night."

"Why did it take so long to get to Manzanillo?"

"The pickup isn't a car. Besides, we had a flat. Look." Nivaldo took a piece of paper from his wallet. "The receipt for the tire. Ask the garage man, he'll remember we got there at ten."

"Where did you have the flat?" Quintero let the man stand there holding out his hand with the receipt.

"Just as we reached the highway, a little before the bridge."

"That's enough! Tell Ramón I want to see him right away."

The little man left. In a few minutes, Quintero saw the pickup disappear in the direction of the dam embankment. He went to the dining room for a cup of coffee, a pot of which the cook kept ready at all times, for the kitchen personnel. The assistant cook, a fat, jolly, black man, said:

"This place is all stirred up! Everybody's being arrested!"

"Not quite everybody, Nicolás!" Quintero said and turned to go.

"Well, from here it looks like nobody who goes in the warehouse ever comes back out."

Quintero left grinning. He noticed that the pickup was returning. A few minutes later he found himself facing a tall, strong, swarthy man abut thirty-five years old, with a mustache and a kind, gentle face. Ramón was the best foreman at the site. He was demanding, able and tireless, and as such, he commanded everyone's respect. Quintero noted the quick glance to the window. The pickup had parked about thirty meters away, on the road to the embankment that led to the site.

"Explain again what you did the night Alberto García died."

"I went to Manzanillo after supper."

"Where did you have a flat tire?"

"Right at the highway."

"That's about two kilometers from here. About twenty minutes on foot at a fair pace, maybe less if you take a short cut through the savannah."

"I haven't measured it."

"How long did it take you to fix the tire?"

"I don't know . . . maybe twenty minutes, half an hour."

"In that case, did you see the Manzanillo bus go by?"

"I . . . don't remember," Ramón's voice had lost its mildness and become hard.

"You never met the victim before you came to the site?"

The muscles of Ramón's face and arms stiffened.

"No!"

"Are you sure?"

"Positive!"

"All right, you can go."

Ramón didn't move. He seemed to be surprised. Finally he turned. When he was almost at the door, Quintero said:

"You never met Lucio Benavides either, did you Gordo?"

Ramón froze, then suddenly whirled and in one movement hurled himself against the desk, slamming it into Quintero who, caught off guard, was knocked to the floor. Ramón grabbed Quintero's pistol and jumped out the window, sprinting toward the pickup that was waiting with the motor running. But there, a surprise was waiting for him. At the wheel, instead of Nivaldo, was a man dressed in olive green. Ramón aimed and squeezed the trigger, but the only sound was the metallic click of the hammer on an empty chamber. At that moment, Quintero appeared with a revolver in his hand.

Romelio, in the driver's seat, said: "Nice going, kid. You nailed him!"

"Just like I said! These troublemakers, when they think they're surrounded, they always try to break out. It never fails!"